T0067151

Indian Agent

ROD SCURLOCK

authorHOUSE®

AuthorHouse™
1663 Liberty Drive
Bloomington, IN 47403
www.authorhouse.com
Phone: 1 (800) 839-8640

Published by AuthorHouse   03/23/2015

ISBN: 978-1-5049-0130-7 (sc)
ISBN: 978-1-5049-0129-1 (e)

Print information available on the last page.

Any people depicted in stock imagery provided by Thinkstock are models,
and such images are being used for illustrative purposes only.
Certain stock imagery © Thinkstock.

This book is printed on acid-free paper.

CHAPTER ONE

The wind was picking up in the west now, sending dust and sand in their faces. It was only a matter of time until the war party would be on them, if they kept going in the same direction.

Tom Colter looked around for the fourth time. It wasn't any different than it had been the last three times. There was no place to get to for protection. They had tied their horses to some trees and climbed the bare ridge to look ahead, and as they crept up to the summit to look over, they almost ran into a small war party of Sioux on the other side. The Indians were too near the summit for them to crawl back without getting spotted. All they could do was lie still in the tall prairie grass, and hope.

Tom looked over at his partner. The big Swede was lying with his face in the sand, the same as he was. It was a fine pickle for two of Brewster's best scouts to find themselves in! From being the hunters, they suddenly found themselves the hunted! He was glad it was Ole who was with him. The big blond had shoulders like a bull, and he was tall and fearless. There had been many scrapes that they had found themselves in, and that easy-going man had stood by his side as they fought their way free. There was no one he would rather have with him now.

Tom chanced another peek over the ridge, being sure to move very slowly so that the motion was not noticed. The Indians had dismounted, and were sitting in a circle, just beyond the crest of the ridge. Tom motioned to Ole to move back, and the two slid down the side of the ridge to the small hollow below them. When they had retreated far enough, they got to their feet and hurried to the grove of juniper where they had tied the horses.

Leading the horses around the grove, they climbed into their saddles. They then moved out, keeping the junipers between them and the Indians as much as possible. When he felt they were sufficiently far enough away, Tom stopped.

"Ole, I think we should take a pasear down this draw and then head on up north a ways, then circle back around for another look at that bunch."

"Ay t'ink you have the holes in the head."

"No, Brewster needs to know if it's just this bunch, or if there's a bigger band hanging around with them."

Ole looked at his partner. Tom was taller and almost as big as he was, with a shock of light brown hair and a ready smile, with laugh lines already showing near his steel-blue eyes. Those eyes right now were saying, we're going to do this.

"Vel, the vorst could happen is ve lose our scalps. Yust lead the vay!"

Tom led the way down into the bottom of the shallow valley, and then turned northward along its length. When he calculated that they had gone far enough to be out of sight of the Indians, he reined his horse up out of the valley to a wide ridge.

Surveying the country ahead carefully, they rode on in a westerly direction. There were no places to hide here. It was open, grass-covered prairie. They could see for miles, and there were no other Indians within sight in this direction.

Tom took one more look around in all directions. "Ole, I think that bunch was all there is. What do you think?"

"Ay t'ink so, as vell. If there vere others, this bunch vouldn't have stopped."

"All right. Let's get back to the troops."

It was nearly dark when the two finally came in sight of the soldiers. Tom led the way down to the creek and then up a little rise to the campfire. Tom held his reins out to the orderly, and walked over to where Lieutenant Sayers was talking to some noncoms. Ole followed him.

Tom saluted. "Lieutenant, we spotted a small band about three miles ahead. All young, and all wearing war paint."

"Were they camped or moving?"

"Hard to say, Sir. They had dismounted and were resting on a hillside. There were no women or children with them."

"How many of them were there?"

"I'd say about twenty-five, maybe a few more."

"Can you find them in the dark?"

"Yes, Sir."

"Very good, Colter. You and Swensen go grab some food. The rest have eaten. We'll plan to leave in two hours."

The food wasn't a lot. Dry biscuits with slabs of beef in between the layers, washed down with some hot coffee that would peel the hair off if it touched your skin. That was standard issue when you were on a "skirmish", Tom reflected.

He finished eating, and pulled some tall grass and set it in front of Dusty. "You finish that, and cool off a little more, and I'll take you down for another drink of water." He wanted to be sure the horse was ready for the night excursion. This horse wouldn't run at the sound of gunfire, and would stand if Tom had to get off. Not all horses would do that.

The corporal found him throwing his saddle on Dusty. "The Lieutenant wants to see you and Swensen."

"Soon's I get my gear on this horse."

Tom found Ole and the two made their way over to where the Lieutenant was briefing his noncoms. When he had finished and dismissed them, he turned to his two scouts.

"Go back to where you found the Indians and scout out the countryside. Then come back and give me the layout. I'll leave in about half an hour, and we'll go straight west from here until we meet you."

The moon drifted out from behind some clouds just as the two came to the ridge where the Indians had been sitting. They ground-reined their horses and crept up the side of the ridge on their bellies. Tom eased himself up to the top, making sure of each movement before moving on, so that no stone rolled, or a twig broke, that would give him away. When he was able to see across the ridge, the Indians were gone!

He sat up and looked down at Ole. "They've vamoosed! Where in the heck do you think they could have gone? It was late in the day. I wouldn't think they went far."

"Yah, the creek is yust about a mile south. You t'ink maybe they vent there?"

"Good thought. You wait here for the Lieutenant. I'll go over to the creek and scout around there. Tell him to wait here until I get back."

They went back to their horses, and Tom climbed into his saddle and rode south. It took him about half an hour to reach the creek. He stopped on a ridge just above the water and scanned the area below him. The moon was now hidden behind some clouds.

Dismounting, Tom started moving around the ridge top, looking for a better view of the creek bottom. He could see the shadows from the cottonwood and willow trees lining the creek. They made it difficult to tell if there were Indians camped there, or not.

He could see the shapes of a monolith and some rocks to his right. He eased over that way to keep from being seen from below if the moon did come out. He stopped at the bottom of the monolith and sat with his back to the stone. The dim outline of the moon was moving toward the edge of a cloud. Soon, he would have a better view of the creek bottom, and could tell for sure if they were down there.

He heard an owl hoot across the valley, and right after that, an answering hoot from just above him on the rock! They had posted sentries! How did he get where he was without being seen or heard, and what did he do now?

Tom eased over onto his side, crawled around to the side of a large boulder, and stood. Maybe if he could get around behind the rock, he could sneak up on the sentry from behind. As he got to the back of the monolith, he saw a pile of rocks that was braced up against it. That was how the Indian got to the top of the monolith. Tom felt his way in the dim light for a way to get on top of the pile.

He found a smaller rock that allowed him to pull himself up on the rock pile. Just as he was reaching the top, his hand came away with a chunk of rock that broke loose when he pulled on it. A bunch of smaller rocks came loose, as well, and went tumbling down the side. It sounded like a roll of thunder to Tom! The Indian grunted, and Tom could hear him walking about on the monolith. Tom froze! He was in no position to fight with him, hanging on the side of that rock.

He looked up at the sky. The moon was getting closer to the edge of the cloud all the time. Very soon it was going to be light all around. Tom hung there without moving until he thought the Indian had quit looking his way, and then inched slowly up to the top of the wide rock pile. He stood up and started toward the monolith. Just then, the moon came out of the clouds and almost daylight flooded the area.

Tom looked up and the Indian was standing right above him with his back to him. The man turned around looking at the country, and then lowered his gaze to where Tom was standing. He started, then, dove off the monolith, crashing onto Tom. They both sailed off the rock pile onto the ground below. The impact knocked the wind out of Tom and he struggled to get his breath.

The Indian pulled his arm loose, trying to get his tomahawk out of his belt. Tom was holding onto him with all his might, trying to breathe. The tomahawk came loose and the Indian raised his arm, intending to bring the weapon down on Tom's head. Tom reached up and grabbed his arm, keeping it from descending onto him.

He got his other arm free and swung a fist into the Indian's chin. He couldn't get enough swing to be effective. Tom butted his head into the other man's face, the blow breaking the Indian's nose. The Indian dropped his weapon and clutched his bleeding face. Tom quickly reached down and grabbed a rock and brought it down hard on the Indian's head. He made sure the man was dead before leaving.

Tom got to his feet, made a quick sashay around the ridgetop, noting the contours of the area, where the creek ran, the direction of a shallow swale that ran down the hill toward the creek, and any other features that he thought would help the Lieutenant. Once he had these in his mind, he ran back to Dusty. He then headed back north to where Ole was waiting.

The patrol was there when he arrived. Tom went right to the Lieutenant. "They are down on the creek and they've posted sentries. I took one out, but I'm sure there are more."

Squatting down by the officer, Tom drew a map in the dirt showing how they could best surround the area without being seen.

The Lieutenant studied the drawing for a time, then, called his noncoms over. He laid out a plan for their foray. "No one is to shoot until I do, unless they're attacked. We'll come in on them from three sides like this," he said, pointing to a spot on the map. "The first squad will wait on the ridge until the others are in place, then we'll come in on them from the three sides at once. I hope to get them to surrender peacefully. Our mission is to bring them in to the fort, and when we have the whole tribe, or at least the main part of it, they'll be transferred to a reservation. If they make a fight of it, of course you will protect yourselves."

They mounted and rode on to the south, the Lieutenant, Tom and Ole leading the group. When they reached the spot where Tom had fought the Indian, the officer stopped and surveyed the area below them. He then dispatched one group to the left, and ordered the noncom in charge of another group to wait until everyone was in place below. He then led the third group down to the right. Tom and Ole rode with them.

When they were in place down near the creek, he motioned for the other groups to proceed. All three started a slow ride in toward the sleeping Indians. Daylight was just appearing over the ridge to the east.

Tom heard an owl hoot several times, and knew they had been discovered. The lieutenant pulled out a white cloth, tied it to his sword and held it over his head. He motioned for Tom and Ole to come with him, and signaled his group to stay back. The other two groups saw what was happening and held back as well.

Some of the Indian chiefs of the Sioux were realizing that their way of life was gone, and that they had to face changes or die. Some were fighting to the end in spite of overwhelming odds. It was the latter that had made it their goal in life to kill every settler they could and destroy everything that belonged to them. Wagon trains and other travelers were every bit as vulnerable to their raids. This is what brought the Army to capture all the Indians they could, with the intent to transfer them to a reservation and hold them there.

Lieutenant Sayers stopped a short distance from the Indian encampment and waited. Tom could see the Indians watching them and milling around. Finally, one Indian with a long headdress, and two others, mounted their horses and rode out to where the soldiers were sitting.

When they got together, the Lieutenant pointed to the east, then the north, and then behind him.

"Chief, we have you surrounded. Please come peacefully. We will take you to the fort and then to a reservation where you and your people can live in peace."

One Indian, who obviously could speak English, sat talking to the chief. They talked for some time. The chief glared at the officer, spat on the ground, took the spear he was holding and slammed it into the grass-covered earth. Then he turned his horse and rode back into his encampment, followed by the other two.

Tom, Ole and the Lieutenant sat their horses, watching the Indian encampment. There was much stirring around there.

Sayers looked at Tom. "What are they doing?

Tom reached into his saddlebag and pulled out his long glass. After a long look at the Indians, he lowered the glass and handed it to the officer. "They're putting on their war paint. There's no surrendering in that bunch."

"What do you recommend we do?"

"Sir, in a very few minutes we're going to be in the damnedest battle you ever saw, no matter what we do. I'd suggest we take the initiative and go in after them."

"Swensen, do you agree?"

"Yah. Ve yust as vell get them before they're ready for us. They still aren't on their horses."

"I think you're right."

Lieutenant Sayers lifted his pistol and shot into the air. Then the three of them charged toward the Indian camp, followed by the three cavalry units. The Indians quickly picked up their weapons, mounted their horses and rode out to meet the charging soldiers.

Horses and men met in the middle, with spears, bows and arrows, and pistols all going at once, and reaping a harvest of riders from both sides.

Tom saw an Indian fletching an arrow and aiming it at him. He quickly flung himself to the right. Hanging over the side, he shot the man from under his horse's neck. Tom and Ole and the other soldiers continued to ride back and forth in the midst of the melee, firing and reloading, and firing some more.

Suddenly the Indians withdrew, and all took a long breath. Maybe that was it. Maybe the Indians would surrender, and they could go back to the fort peacefully, with the remaining Indians in tow.

The Indians gathered in a tight group around the chief with the flowing head gear. Suddenly, they gave a loud, blood-curdling yell, and once again rode headlong toward Tom and the group of soldiers he was with.

A long line of Indians spread out across the low intervening ridge. Spears, bows and arrows, and some muskets were visible as the line charged toward them.

Tom could feel a tightening in his stomach that was always there when they were about to enter into a close-fought battle. Tom checked the loads in his pistol for the third time.

Tom saw the chief coming in his direction, and he fired at him. The Indian winced, and then continued to come at him. Another Indian was riding toward Tom from the left, wielding a tomahawk. Tom shifted his gun toward the man and fired. The Indian jerked back but then straightened up again, and kept coming. He was a horse-length in front of the chief when Tom fired twice more at him. Tom knew he was hitting him. He was too close to miss, but it didn't stop him. The Indian had a wild look in his eye, and was holding his tomahawk high, attempting to bring it down on Tom.

Tom fired once more and the Indian toppled forward, the arc of the tomahawk coming down on Tom's shoulder.

Tom turned his attention back to the chief. The man had his spear held high, ready to throw it. Tom swung his pistol around and pulled the trigger again, but his gun was empty.

The chief bore down on him, and before Tom could leap at the man to bring him off his horse, the chief threw his spear. Tom felt a huge pain in his left leg, and looked down to see the spear head sticking out the back side of his leg.

He was seized with a sudden impulse to vomit, and every step his horse took sent a sharp rush of pain up his leg. He moved over to the side of the battle and pulled Dusty to a halt. The pain was overwhelming.

Looking up, Tom saw that the Indians hadn't stayed to fight, but were running their horses at full speed on toward the mountains to the west, the soldiers following them at full gallop.

Tom looked down at the spear. He couldn't move his leg to dismount. All he could do was try to hold up the handle of the spear to take some pressure off his leg. A couple of soldiers from one of the other groups stopped to help the wounded. They noticed Tom sitting there, and rode over. One, a sergeant, saw Tom's leg and dismounted. He and his partner helped him off his horse and laid him down on the ground.

The sergeant took out his knife and cut away Tom's pant leg, and looked at the spear. "We can't pull it out. That would tear up a lot more flesh than you've lost so far. We've got to break that handle and pull it out forward by the spearhead. There isn't any way to do it easy."

Tom gritted his teeth. "Do what you have to, but do it fast."

The sergeant pointed to the group coming back from chasing the Indians. "Go get the lieutenant, and ask him to bring his sword over here. We need it."

When the officer got there, the sergeant placed his own hand between the handle of the spear and Tom's leg. "This is going to hurt like hell, but it's the best we can do here. Lieutenant, take the sword and hack into that handle just above where it enters his leg. Stop when you're almost through and maybe we can break it off the rest of the way. All right, Tom, I wish we had some whiskey or something, but put this stick in your mouth so you don't break a tooth. Now, Sir, let's get it done."

Lieutenant Sayers got around on the other side of Tom, pulled out his sword and took aim at the wood. The sword bit in to the wood a short way, and Tom passed out with the pain.

Seeing this, the sergeant said, "That's good. At least he won't feel any more of it. Let's stay with it."

They finished hacking through the spear handle and then pulled the spear on through the leg. They bound the wound, and laid Tom back on the ground.

Lieutenant Sayers looked around him. Two more injured soldiers besides Colter, and what looked like about seven dead Indians lying there, and he had nothing to show for it all. He was supposed to capture the Indians and bring them back to the fort to transport to some reservation. Col. Brewster would very likely have some choice words for him over this.

He looked at all six feet of Colter lying there, all the way from the unruly brown thatch of hair to the bottom of his boots. He was a big man, wide-shouldered and muscular. How was he going to get him and the other wounded back to the fort? Tom would never be able to sit a saddle with that wound in his thigh. The officer went around to check on the other wounded.

Ole Swensen came over to where Tom was lying, and sat down. When Tom woke up, he looked up at Ole. "Did they get it out?"

"Slicker'n a vistle," he grinned. "And you didn't lose more than two or three quarts of blood. Now you'd better get up and valk back to the fort. You aren't goin' to sit in your saddle vith that vound. Vait right here."

Ole walked into the woods nearby and returned with two poles, each about twelve feet long. "Here, let me help you sit up. Now give me your coat."

Ole helped Tom get his coat off, and then shucked his own. Then he strung the poles through the sleeves of the two coats and buttoned both coats around the poles, forming a travois. Then they sat talking about the raid until the Lieutenant came back.

Sayers looked down at the coats. "What have you got here, Swensen?"

"It's kind of a travois, Sir. Would you have a couple of troopers lead our horses? I'll sit on my horse and hold the ends of the two poles. He can ride on the travois."

"An excellent idea, Swensen. I think we'll try that with the rest of the wounded."

When they had more of the travois rigged up for the worst of the wounded, the Lieutenant led the way back toward the fort, followed by Ole, then the other wounded, and the able-bodied troopers brought up the rear.

Every bounce on a rock or stick brought a shot of pain to Tom's leg. It was pure agony, and the trip seemed interminable. Ole's shoulders were feeling like they were being pulled out of their sockets from the constant pull backwards of the loaded travois. The other soldiers with the same job were also having the problem. Lieutenant Sayers stopped often to give the men a little relief.

The shadows were growing long when the cavalcade pulled into the fort. Sayers sent a man to fetch the doctor, and the rest packed the wounded into the doctor's office.

When the doctor arrived, Sayers told him about the men's wounds, and then made his way to the Colonel's office to report. He dreaded telling him that he had wounded, and didn't bring a single Indian in to be moved to a reservation.

Ole Swensen came into the doctor's office and was immediately put to work helping. When they got to Tom, they got his pants off and the doctor unwrapped the makeshift bandage that had been applied in the field.

"Son, you have a bad wound for a cavalry man. I don't think you'll sit a saddle for a day or two. Well, let's see what we can do with it." He gave Tom a shot of laudanum, cleaned out the wound, sewed it up, and rebandaged it. "Now let's look at that shoulder."

Tom had forgotten the tomahawk swipe to his shoulder. It was minor, and the doctor soon had it sewed up. The doctor patted Tom on the shoulder. "You'll live, but you'll have a pretty long rest ahead of you."

Tom spent the next two weeks in the doctor's ante-room. Ole came in during the evenings when he wasn't out on patrol, telling him of the day's adventures.

This evening was growing long. Tom was impatient to get out. His leg was better, and Doc had let him stand today. It hurt like fire, but he had to get out of that bed! He looked up as Ole came through the door.

"Well, how many Indians did you capture today?"

"Vell, I yust captured fifty today, the others yust stood and vatched."

"Well, we can't all be heroes. You brought in fifty today?"

"Yah."

"The fort must be filling up. What are they going to do with them all?"

"Ay tink they're yust about ready to ship 'em out."

"I'm ready to get out of here, and get on my horse and see some country."

"Ay tink if you get on your horse now, you vould be the wrong end of the horse!"

Two more days passed. Doc was letting him sit up in a chair now. It still hurt like blazes to sit on that leg, but it was healing, and he knew he would soon be able to get around, but time sure went by slow. He sat looking out the window and wishing he was out there doing something.

The door opened and Colonel Brewster walked in. "Hello, soldier, how are you doing?"

Tom pushed on the sides of the chair, trying to stand. Brewster held up his hand. "Don't try to stand, Colter. I'm just glad to hear you are doing so well. You had quite a wound."

"Yes, Sir, but I think I'm ready to get back to work."

"Well, that isn't what the doctor said, but he did say you were a lot better. Colter, I want to talk to you about a reassignment. As you know, we are going to transport these Indians to a reservation. The one they're going to is new. There are no in-place facilities there, just bare ground. I need to put someone in charge there that I can trust. You are my best scout, and I hate to lose you there, but I've just got to have someone take over this new reservation that I can count on to keep it in order, and to get the Indians to settle down on that chunk of ground. It won't be an easy task."

"I appreciate the confidence, Sir, but what do I know about herding a bunch of Indians? All I know is how to find them in a battle."

"The reason you can do that is that you know their habits, way of life, and how they think. That's just what I need right now. Will you do it? There's a field promotion to Lieutenant for you, in it."

"How many Indians are we talking about?"

"That depends on how successful Sayers is in rounding up the rest. There will be between three and five hundred, I'd imagine."

"If I understand you right, I would have to hold three hundred Indians, who don't want to be there, on a chunk of ground, see that they're fed and clothed, and take care of their problems. Is that anywhere near the case?"

"That's about it, Colter. I just don't have anyone that I think can do the job as well as you can. Will you do it? I could order you to, but I would like to have you go willingly."

"What do I have for a crew?"

"I'll detail a squad to move the Indians to the reservation, and leave the soldiers there for six months. By that time, you should have some sort of police system set up to maintain order and keep them on the reservation."

"Could I have Swensen, as well?"

"I hate to lose both of my best scouts, but if that will help you accept the job, I'll let him go, too. Also, I will assign a quartermaster to take care of the provisions. That will leave you free to handle the Indian problems, and keep them in place until they have decided that is where they have to stay. That will be a full-time job."

"Well, Colonel, against my better judgment, I'll take the job. I just hope that I can do it."

"Tom, it's a strange world we live in. We are hired to protect the citizens of this country. The pioneers have moved out into this wilderness, along with miners, trappers, and outlaws, all trying to make a living for themselves. They have moved into lands that the Indians took centuries ago, when they arrived here. The Indians, rather than trying to see if there is a way we can live together, have taken to raiding and killing the settlers. Then it becomes our responsibility to stop their raiding, and we wind up going to war with them to protect the settlers.

"As a result, we wind up with a host of old men, women and children, and some able-bodied men that we have captured, that we have to do something with. We have no choice but to put them on a reservation and hold them there, to keep them from raiding the settlers in their homes. Of course they resent this, and hate us for it. Yours won't be an easy task. Very good, Lieutenant Colter. I don't know anyone who could do it better." He rose, shook Tom's hand. "Get well soon." Then he left the room.

Tom returned to his cot, and lay there thinking about the new assignment. He could feel the weight of it like a crushing monster pushing him right into the ground. Where in heck do you start? He rolled it over and over in his head. He had never been faced with anything like this before. Finally, he fell asleep.

He was awakened by the door slamming, and opened his eyes to Ole Swensen coming through the door, dressed in a top sergeant's uniform.

He marched straight into the room, stopped, brought his feet together, then smartly turned left toward the bed, then marched smartly to the side of the bed, turned once more toward Tom, stopped, brought his feet together with a click, and saluted.

"First Sergeant Olaf Walfred Swensen reporting for duty, Sir!" He formally brought his hand back to his side, and stood there at attention with a grin a mile wide on his face.

Tom lay there, laughing. "Your first order, Sergeant, is to wipe that silly smirk off your face. What are you doing in that uniform?"

Ole sat down on the edge of the bed. "I had a visit from the Colonel. He tells me I have been made a first sergeant and that we are going to babysit a bunch of Indians. How did that happen?"

"He told me that you were so ornery that he couldn't stand the disruption you caused to the troops all the time, and that I was to go along and try to keep you under control. I told him that was impossible. He said he knew that, but I was to do the best I could."

"Vell, Ay told him that now you vere an officer, Ay vouldn't be able to stand the sight of you and your svelled head. Vat do ve do now?"

"Get me out of bed the first thing."

CHAPTER TWO

The next two weeks started with Tom walking around the room on crutches with the doctor's, and then Ole's, help. After that, he was able to get by with a cane and able to walk outside, to the mess hall and to the main office. The colonel had a desk brought in to the room next to his office.

One morning, Tom was ordered to report to the main office. He donned his clothes and reported to the colonel.

Brewster came around the desk and shook his hand. "I'm glad to see you up and around and ready to go to work. The first thing, Lieutenant - you are badly out of uniform. I realize that you have always carried out your duties in your buckskins, but now you are in charge of a squad of soldiers, and with that goes the uniform that they have been taught to obey without question. I'll expect to see that taken care of."

"Yes, Sir."

Tom started working on the details for the trip to the reservation, arranging for supplies for the troops, the Indians, and for the means of transporting all of it. Ole and Sergeant Bull Bascomb were his legs, and saw to the details. It was a strange feeling, sitting at a desk all day, working out the particulars of what would be needed, and then having someone else take care of putting it all together. A far cry from the free and easy life he and Ole had been used to. Instead of the wide open spaces with their expansive grasslands, timbered mountains and clear running streams, he spent his days looking at four walls and mountains of paper.

One day, Colonel Brewster came out to Tom's desk. "Do you feel you have all the arrangements made for the trip?"

"To the best of my knowledge, Sir."

"Then let's plan on starting day after tomorrow. It's getting hard to hold the Indians in these cramped quarters.

"Here's a rough sketch of the reservation. There is desert on two sides, east and west. To the south is a mountain range, and on the north a tall mountain. Terrain on the reservation itself comprises some of all of it. I've heard some say we are giving them land nobody else wants, but I think you'll find they can make their living there better than the non-Indians that have moved into the flatlands beside it. I haven't seen it myself, but that is what the reports have said. Good luck."

The morning air was crisp. Lt. Thomas James Colter was decked out in his new uniform. He felt conspicuous as he stepped out into the parade grounds. He had worked with these troops for years now, they were good friends, and suddenly it appeared different. Now he was their commanding officer. How were they going to react to this? He hobbled over to where the supply wagons were standing. They were loaded, and several of the troops were just now bringing the horses over to hitch them to the wagons.

Sergeant Bull Bascomb came up from the building where the Indians were being held. He saluted. "Sergeant Bascomb reporting, Sir."

Tom returned the salute. He started to say "Is everything ready, Bull?", but he checked himself. "Very good, Sergeant. Are the Indians ready to travel?"

"As ready as we can get them, Sir. Several of the men are wounded from skirmishes, and there are two sick children."

"Have they been fed?"

"Yes, Sir."

"All right. Find a place for the sick children in one of the wagons, and an Indian woman to stay with them. If the wounded warriors have leg wounds, find a place for them, also. Bring them all out when the wagons are hitched up, and prepare to travel in a half-hour."

"Yes, Sir." The sergeant saluted and turned back to the building.

Tom looked at the six wagons, all stacked with supplies: farm implements, carpenter tools, kitchen equipment, and who knew what else. On top of that, there would be three hundred and forty six Sioux Indians. All he had to do was get them across one hundred miles of wild, unsurveyed land to where none of them wanted to go. He hobbled back to the main office, and went in.

Colonel Brewster was seated at his desk. Tom walked into the room and saluted. "The caravan is ready to leave, Sir."

The Colonel returned the salute. "Are you sure you are physically ready, Tom?"

"Physically ready, Sir? Yes, Sir. Just bed sores from that blamed bed. I'm not so sure mentally. When I look at the wagons loaded out there, and then think that there will be almost three hundred and fifty mad Indians trailing them, it gets a little overwhelming."

"A soldier by the name of Fister will be coming in soon with some supplies. He will bring some cattle, also. I'm hoping we can get you fifty head, or so. Some of the cattle you will need for immediate consumption, and we'll try to have more in another month. We'll try to keep you supplied, but we have trouble just keeping the fort provisioned, so you might want to keep that in mind. Keep me informed, Tom, and I'll try to help all I can. You've got one hell of a job ahead of you. Good luck, and God be with you."

Good luck to me, Tom thought, it's going to take a lot more than luck, I have a feeling. Thirty soldiers to keep three hundred and fifty

Indians corralled, especially when those Indians would like to shoot you, and certainly don't want to be herded across country like a bunch of sheep!

Ole came up with the saddled Dusty and tied him to the back of the first wagon, then came up and helped Tom into the wagon seat. Corporal Matt Southern climbed up beside Tom and took the reins. Ole retrieved his horse and rode up alongside. "Your caravan is ready, Sir."

Tom looked back. Five heavily-laden wagons were strung out behind him. Behind them, was one big bunch of Indians, kept in line by twenty-five mounted cavalrymen. Soldiers were lined up on the porches of the buildings and along the walls, watching the procession.

Tom looked at the big log gates of the fort. What was waiting for him on the other side of those gates? He had been through them many times, looking forward to his trip ahead, riding out in front of a detail, with new country to explore. This time was far different!

Colonel Brewster came out of the office, walked over to Tom's wagon and saluted. "Good luck, Tom."

Tom returned the salute. "Thank you, Sir. I think we'll need it."

He raised his arm and motioned the cavalcade forward. He had an uneasy feeling as they passed through the gates. Now all of this was his to deal with! He pointed to the west and Matt turned the horses in that direction.

"Matt, just keep them at a slow pace. Some of those older people and the little children may have a hard time keeping up. It will be tough enough on them as it is, before we're there. We'll stop every hour for a ten-minute rest."

Fortunately, the terrain was fairly level the first day, but every rock they went over gave Tom a jolt in his leg. He called a halt when they came to a small stream. The sun was reaching its zenith, his leg was hurting, and he was stiff from bouncing around in the wagon all morning. He knew the Indians must be tired. Tom got down from the wagon, just as Sergeant Bascomb was coming up.

"Let's stop here, Sergeant. We'll feed the Indians first, and then the rest of you eat. Keep half the men on watch while the other half eats. We'll rest here for two hours."

Tom walked back to check on the meal. Two of the soldiers were at the back of the food supply wagon handing out sandwiches that had been prepared at the fort to the line of Indians that were strung out behind. Two others were passing canteens around, and then refilling them from the water barrel. The Indians were accepting the food, and then going back and sitting in their original position in the march.

Tom waited to eat until the others had their food. Ole joined him, sitting in the shade of his wagon. Tom said, "Ole, do you think everything is going all right?"

"Smooth as silk, so far."

"Would you put on your scout hat from now on, and ride out front? I don't want any surprises if I can help it. Matt can go with you, and I'll drive the wagon. There may be stray war parties, or outlaws for that matter, that would salivate over some of these supplies. Look for a camp spot for tonight while you're out there."

Once underway again, Tom watched Ole and Matt ride off in front. It seemed strange. That's where he should be. Out with Ole on a scout, instead of sitting here driving a team of horses. Life was strange sometimes. He pulled back on the reins. The team was starting to walk too fast.

Tom looked back continually to try to judge how the Indians were faring on their march. They were stretched out for what seemed miles, the women helping the younger children over the rougher spots. The soldiers were riding back and forth along the line, keeping it moving, but without pushing them too hard.

Tom tried to maintain a pace that kept the column moving, but not so fast that the women and children had trouble keeping up.

The afternoon wore on much the same as the morning had passed. Just a slow procession of the six wagons, followed by the line of marching Indians, with the soldiers spread out along the sides guarding them.

The dust rose in clouds from the horse's feet and settled on the contents of the wagons, including those driving them. Tom looked back and could see that the long column of walkers was raising dust, as well. It had to be tough walking in that, but he couldn't think of any alternative. He tried to make their way in the grassy areas where he could. He attempted to keep the column moving over terrain as level as possible and still keep in the direction he needed to go.

In the middle of the afternoon, Sergeant Bascomb rode up and signaled to Tom to stop. Tom pulled the horses to a halt. "Have we got a problem, Sergeant?"

"Yes, Sir, there's an older Indian lady that isn't able to keep up and we're about out of room in the wagons. She's the chief's wife."

"Bring her up here and put her on the seat with me. If there are others, see if you can find room in one of the wagons. If need be, we'll call a halt. We don't want to unless it's necessary in order to keep everyone in the line."

Bascomb soon reappeared with the elderly Indian woman. Tom and the sergeant helped her up into the wagon and to get seated on the wide, wooden seat. She sat there staring ahead, looking neither to the right or left. Bascomb motioned to go on ahead and Tom started the team moving forward.

Bascomb rode out in the lead, now that the country was getting undulating and a little rougher, picking out the best routes to avoid uneven ground, wet areas, or other obstructions.

As the afternoon wore on, the sun was right in their faces. The Indian woman would not look any way but straight ahead, and started holding her hand over her eyes to shade them. Tom took off his broad-brimmed hat and put it on her head. She got a big grin on her face. The rest of the day she looked around, enjoying the scenery, and even spent some time studying Tom as they rode.

It was nearly dusk when Tom spotted Ole waving at him and motioning to follow him to the camp site he had picked out. It was down near a small stream. There were cottonwood and willow trees growing along the water, providing plenty of wood for their fires. There was a large, flat area where everyone could bed down.

They pulled up the wagons, unhitched the horses and hobbled them near the stream where there was grass. The soldiers soon had fires going and six large cook pots heating for the slumgullion that was to be the evening meal.

When everyone was fed, Tom called his noncoms up to his wagon. "Ole, what did you find ahead?"

"Ve found two cabins raided. Vun had two dead, and the other vas yust ransacked. It might have been Indian raiders, but Ay don't t'ink so. It looked to me like they vere some kind of outlaw bunch. It looked like about ten horses, maybe eleven. Ve buried the two, a man and a voman."

"What's the trail like ahead?"

"Maybe a little rougher than you've had. It shouldn't slow you down any. There's vun pretty good river to cross, Ay t'ink about tomorrow's stop. The next day should be fairly easy going."

"That sounds good. I'll be glad when we're finally there. Bascomb, will there be a problem keeping guard overnight? Your soldiers will be stretched pretty thin if you have to split the watch hours."

"We have six fires, and we'll put one man at each fire, and a couple roving. I think the Indians are tired enough that there isn't a lot of desire to go wandering. We've issued blankets, and some have wrapped up in them already."

"Good. I think I'm going to follow their example. I'll see you gentlemen in the morning."

Tom and Ole laid their blankets out under Tom's wagon. Ole sat there with a grin on his face. "I never thought I'd see the day. You're sounding like an officer already!"

Tom pulled off his boot and threw it at him.

The next day progressed like the first. Tom and his lady companion were able to converse a little through sign language, and she became almost animated at times. Tom thought maybe he had made a friend. She did keep his hat, though. Tom decided he had lost that.

The noon meal over, they started the trek again. The Indians developed a sort of traveling order, pretty much staying in the same formation, and just putting one foot in front of the other as they traveled. The patrolling soldiers had little to do but ride alongside and watch for any problems.

Tom could see the river from the ridge they were crossing. It made a sharp line against the brown of the prairie, as it wound around small hills and outcrops. It was quite a ways away, but he could tell it was larger than any they had crossed so far. Was this going to be a major problem?

Again, as they approached the river, Ole was up there ahead waving them in. They stopped in the flattened area that Ole had selected.

Tom looked the area over. "Bascomb, I have a question. I believe that we should take the wagons across, unload three of them, and bring them back to haul the Indians across. There's no way they're going to wade that river. What do you think?"

"I don't see any other choice, Sir. I'll assign four troopers to go with the wagons to unload. We'll hold the Indians here until they get that done."

"Ole, did you ride the ford? No quicksand or soft spots?"

"Matt and I rode through it several times. Ay t'ink she's solid."

"Then let's do it."

He climbed back into his wagon and turned the horses toward the water. The horses were at first reluctant to enter the water, but Tom held them to it, slapping them with the tail ends of the reins. The water kept getting deeper the further they went, until it was lapping at the floor of the wagon. A wave came down and surged up over the sides, getting both him and the Indian lady wet. She grabbed Tom's arm and held on tight. He grinned at her, and she grinned back. She was one to travel the road with!

Several times Tom could feel the wagon wheels leave the river bottom and get carried away just a little by the current. Tom's heart jumped into his throat. Were they going to get swept downstream by that swift water? From where he sat, the current was swirling around the wagon bed. It was pounding against the upstream side of the wagon, shaking it and moving it sideways. It just felt to him as if they were floating, or at least on the verge of it. Just the slightest more depth to the water would send them on downstream!

The wheels caught again and he was able to proceed across. He could feel his companion relax as they climbed onto the far shore.

Tom pulled on up to a fairly large, flat place that he felt would hold their entire encampment, and stopped. The other wagons came along right behind him. Climbing down off the wagon, Tom reached up and lifted the lady down. Then he hobbled back to see to the unloading of the three wagons.

Sergeant Bascomb was there supervising the unloading, and the three wagons were soon on their way back across the river for the Indians. Tom watched as the soldiers got the Indians loaded, and soon the three wagons were on their way back toward them. He wondered how the Indians would react to the ride, but when they were well on their way across, it looked to him like they enjoyed the experience, and the children were having a great time.

The soldiers repeated the crossing time after time until all the Indians were on the other side.

There was a great deal of animated discussion around the campfires that evening about the day's activities. The Indians seemed to be accepting their fate more and more as they went. Three more days! He called his noncoms together to discuss the day's trip and what lay ahead.

"It seems that the Indians are becoming more accepting of their situation. What do you think, Bascomb?"

"Yes, Sir, we're having less trouble all the time keeping them together."

"Óle, what's ahead for tomorrow?"

"Easy terrain. Ve go through the timber to get there. It may be more difficult for the soldiers to keep the Indians corralled. Ve go past the ransacked homesteads. That bunch of outlaws may still be around."

"Sergeant, what about going through the timber? Is this going to cause you more problems?"

"We'll just bunch 'em closer together. It'll be all right."

"Good, then I'll see you all at daybreak."

The next morning, dust rose in a column as Tom watched Ole and Matt recede into the distance. He hobbled back past the wagons. He'd sure be glad when he could throw away his cane and walk again! The leg was getting better. He could put his weight on it now, but there was still a lot of pain.

The horses were all hitched to the wagons, and the Indians were standing and waiting. Bascomb waved his hand that they were ready. Tom walked back to his wagon, lifted Maple Leaf into the wagon. At least, that was the name he thought she was signing to him. He climbed aboard himself and picked up the reins. Once more, his caravan was underway.

He could tell as the day progressed that they were gaining altitude. It was cooler, and the vegetation was changing, as well. North slopes had trees on now, and as the day went on, the trees were larger and soon were on all of the slopes. They were in the timber country now. The trees were mostly ponderosa pine, and on south-facing slopes pinon pine.

Their trail continued to rise for the next two days, winding through the timber, open meadow areas and grassy slopes.

On the morning of the fifth day, Tom saw Ole wending his way through the denser timber ahead, and waved to him to come back.

"Ole, maybe you and Bascomb had better stay in closer and pick a way through these trees for us. The troops have the Indians bunched in pretty close, but we may hit a place where we can't get a wagon through, and then we'd have the problem of trying to get back. They follow the wagons pretty well when they're moving, but if we have to turn back, it might be a problem getting them gathered and moving ahead of the wagons. Kind of like pushing a log chain uphill."

Ole, Matt and Bascomb stayed in closer, and picked a path through the timber that the wagons could navigate. Once, Tom thought they had made a mistake. The trees looked too close to pass between them, but when he got up to them, there was barely clearance to negotiate between the trees. Tom breathed a sigh of relief, and thanked the competence of the three men.

They climbed to a summit in the ridge they were ascending, and Tom called a halt for lunch and a rest. It was open here, with sandstone rock covering most of the area.

Tom helped Maple Leaf down and found some sandwiches for both of them. They sat down together to eat. Before he had finished eating, Tom saw Ole and Matt coming back up the trail from the west. He stood to meet them.

"What's the matter? You seem to be in a hurry."

"Tom, do you remember an outlaw gunman by the name of Seth Ballinger?"

"Yes, I remember him well. He's a bad one."

"He and about twenty-five of his men are right behind us. They jumped us down the trail, and ve had to hightail it to get away from them. They'll be here in a few minutes."

"Maybe with all the soldiers, they won't dare tackle us."

"Ay don't t'ink so. He loves to fight. He'll do it if he t'inks he can get avay vith it."

Tom looked up and saw a bunch of riders coming up the trail. "Ole, tell Bascomb what's happening, but tell him to keep enough soldiers back there to hold the Indians. We can't let them get loose at this point. Bring up the ones that he can spare."

Tom stood waiting for the outlaws to approach. A large bearded man with ice-cold eyes rode up to Tom and dismounted.

"Soldier, what have we here?" He looked closer at Tom. "Hey! Aren't you Tom Colter? What are you doing in that monkey suit? Have you gone soft?"

"Hello, Seth. No, just another assignment. What are you doing here?"

Seth waved his hand toward the bunch of hard cases that had formed a circle around Tom, Ole, and the soldiers. "You see, Tom, the boys and I have run into some hard times. We thought we'd take a look at what you had here, and maybe we could use some of the things you're packing." He laughed. "Just for old time's sake, you understand."

Tom looked over the crew of men. They were a tough-looking bunch all right. Their clothes were well-worn and dirty. All of the men had beards, and all of them were armed. Many of the pistols were tied down, indicating they were gunmen. The holsters were oiled and appeared to have had much use.

"Sorry, Seth. None of this is for sale. You'll have to look elsewhere"

"Well, now, Tom. That's not neighborly at all." He waved his hand for some of his men to circle around a little further.

Tom held up his hand. "Stop right now. You're not going any further!"

"Tom, we're comin' in, and we're goin' to take what we need. Them soldier boys ain't gonna stop us. I've got twenty-five fast guns here, all around you. You haven't got a chance."

"Seth, I know that you can kill me, maybe a bunch of the soldiers, but they are seasoned troopers, and you won't get all of them. They will take a big toll on your crew. But think on this. I can outdraw you, and I am concentrating on you. Even if you shoot me, I will kill you. You can count on that. Now, you can leave peaceably and we won't fire on you. Your choice."

The outlaw chief looked at Tom several minutes, then looked up to his crew. Tom could tell that he was weighing the odds.

"All right, Tom, you've called this shot, but there'll be another day." He climbed on his horse and led the others back down the trail.

Ole walked over to where Tom was standing.

"Yeeumpin Yeehosophats! Ay' thought ve vere goin' to do battle right there. He's one tough hombre. Ay' never thought he vould back down. Not in front of all of his men!"

Sergeant Bascomb walked up and saluted. "Lieutenant, I salute you. That took a lot of sand. I will tell you that there'll never be a time when any man in this squadron won't stand right beside you in any kind of conflict."

"Well, Sergeant, let's get the people fed and get on down the hill."

The trail led down through the timber, with patches of clearing now and then. It was darker in under all the trees, and Tom was surprised that the sun's rays were long when they finally came out of the timber and into a valley filled with meadow grass, and with a small stream running right down the middle.

Ole and Matt were standing in a flat area on the right side of the creek. Tom pulled his wagon up beside them. "Are we home?"

Matt grinned. "Yep, this is it. I was here when the reservation was selected. You made it!"

Tom helped Maple Leaf out of the wagon and she walked back to where the Indians were gathering.

Tom looked around. "I'm really glad to have this trip over, but I have a hunch the work is just about to begin."

Soon, the fires were going and the slumgullion was cooking. Tom sat on his wagon tongue, looking over the country side. The trail where the wagons sat was on a bench a short way above the bottom of the valley, with a fairly deep, slow-moving creek running through it. A very high hill rose up about three hundred feet from the wagon on the north side. It was grass-covered at the bottom, rising to a wide bench, then, rising again a few hundred feet to another slightly smaller bench, and from there, stretched for what looked to be to the sky. The upper portion was covered with small pinon pines and smaller brush.

To the west, the valley dropped away to the desert, miles away. Tall cottonwood and willow lined the creek as it wandered down the valley. Sagebrush covered the further reaches from the creek, until the hills rose on either side.

To the south, the valley extended for a mile or more before rising to the timbered hills beyond it. The valley itself was covered with tall lush grass.

On the east side was the timbered hillside they had just come down. This was a pretty-well protected valley from the ravages of inclement weather. It should be a good location for the reservation headquarters.

Ole came up and sat beside him. "Vat's first?"

"I was just looking at how we should get going. We have the summer ahead of us, but I think we are pretty high, and we'll need buildings this winter. That first bench up there on the north side will be just right for the supply warehouse. That has to be the first building to protect the supplies.

"We'll put the barns down on the meadow where there's a lot of grass for the stock. Then, I think we'll put up a large warehouse-type building for the Indians. We'll not be able to build tepees for all of them before winter, and those that we can't get shelters for, can stay in the tribal building until we can get the tepees built for them. We'll grab a corner of the warehouse for our use until we can get some of these more essential buildings up. Any suggestions?"

"Ay t'ink you've been doing some t'inking on the vay over. It should vork."

CHAPTER THREE

The first morning at the new location was dreary. A fog bank rolled into the valley, and the Indians stayed close by the fire for the most part, with a few brave souls doing a little exploring close by. The children quickly found a place to play down next to the creek.

Tom called Ole and Bascomb together for a conference. "Sergeant, I'm going to have to appoint one Indian to act as chief for them, so we have a contact to work through. Do you have any suggestions?'

"There is one older man that I noticed they all seem to hold pretty high. He might be a place to start. He has a daughter that speaks English. She's the one who asked for a ride for the older woman."

"Good, bring them up when we get through here. Now, we're going to need one of the soldiers to act as a leader for the building crew, one to manage the stock when it gets here and the horses, also. We'll need one to take care of feeding the Indians, one to oversee the farming, and one to look after sickness or other problems that might come up with the Indians. You can assign the other soldiers to these crews as you can spare them from guard duty. We're going to put together some Indian crews to work with them."

"Pardon me if I think you're crazy, Sir, to try to get them to do that kind of work."

"You may be right, Sergeant, but I'm hoping that I can convince your chief that it's in their best interests to do it. Also, your soldiers will still have the responsibility for keeping them on the reservation. I want you to act as police chief for the present, and it will be your job to organize a tribal police department and train them to be policemen. You can deploy the soldiers as you see fit.

"I'm going to try to talk to the chief today and get recommendations from him as to which Indians we might get to do these jobs. I'm hoping I can get his cooperation. You should sit in on this meeting, too, Bull, and see who he might think will make policemen. Have one of the soldiers bring the chief up here.

"Ole, why don't you take on the job of unloading all of this stuff and covering it with tarps until we can do something better with it. Get a couple of men from Bascomb. Bull, contact the chief and see if you can arrange a meeting with him and his daughter right away. Any questions?"

Bascomb stood up. "Just one, Sir. What did you ever do to rate this assignment? If I ever saw an impossible job, this is it."

"We'll get it done. All right, pick out your building man first, and send him to me."

Tom walked back to his wagon and then stood leaning against it and looking at the terrain, trying to pick out the building sites, and how they would fit in with the eventual agency complex. Bascomb was right. It could get a little overwhelming if he let it.

A soldier came up and saluted. He was a fairly young man, and had a ready smile. "You wished to see me, Sir?"

"What is your name, soldier?"

"Andrew, Sir. Andrew Thoreson"

"You know something about carpentry?"

"Yes, Sir. I worked with a carpenter before I enlisted."

"Good. We are going to try to find some Indians who will work with you. The first job is to build a large warehouse to hold all these supplies, plus what we may have coming, and keep it out of the weather. It will have to be a log structure. There's not much else to build with right now. Can you handle that?"

"Yes, Sir."

"Good, get your plans together and we'll get the men to you as soon as we can identify them."

Tom hoped the other assignments would go this well. Well, that was one. Just as he was congratulating himself on that one, a soldier with an older Indian and a young woman came toward him. The soldier saluted.

"Sir, this is Horse Capture and his daughter. Sergeant Bascomb said to bring them up here."

"Thanks, Private, you can leave them here."

He waved to some sacks of grain near the wagon. "Please sit down. I'm sorry I don't have better accommodations."

The woman spoke to the older man and they took a seat on the grain. Tom sat on one of the sacks, as well.

"I asked Sergeant Bascomb to find someone from the tribe that could speak English so we could set up some kind of communication. Do you speak English?"

He spoke to the man, but the woman looked up and answered, "I do."

"How does it happen that you have this ability?"

"My mother was taken prisoner in a raid when I was a child. Chief Capture took her as his wife. She taught me to speak English."

Looking at her more closely for the first time, Tom said, "You are not Indian?"

"No," she replied, "My parents were settlers and my father was killed in the raid, and my mother, brother, and I were taken to their village. I have come to accept their ways."

"Did you have other family?"

"Not that I know of. Just my brother."

"Would you be willing to act as my interpreter? I can pay you some, although it won't be a lot. My budget is pretty limited."

"Yes, if it is all right with my father."

The older man had a frown on his face. He talked forcefully to the woman. She responded, and then turned to Tom. "My father asks why have you called us here?"

"I need your help. We need to erect buildings, build fences and many other things as quickly as possible. We need to have the Indian men give us a hand."

She repeated this to the man. He again spoke forcefully, using gestures that seemed to Tom were not favorable to his request.

She turned back to Tom. "He says why should we help you? You have fought us, killed women and children, torn down our villages, then herded us into pens like animals, and then made us walk many miles to get here. Why should we help you?"

"Tell him it is for the good of the Indians as much, if not more than, for us. This first building is to keep the food and other supplies that you are going to need dry and safe until it is dispersed. Without it, the supplies would be ruined and there would be nothing to feed you. We will build a building to hold the livestock that we get until it can be given out to everyone. We will start a police force comprised of tribal people to keep everyone safe. Also, tell him I want him to get three or four of his wisest men to act as spokesmen for the people. They will have a voice in what we do.

"I know there is no good feeling toward us. I understand how you feel. I've been sent here to make a place for you all to live, and I will try to make

35

it as pleasant for you as I can. I have no choice but to keep you here, but if we can work together, maybe we can make the best of this situation."

The woman talked at great length to the man. Tom watched her as the exchange was going on. She was quite attractive. She had long, shining dark-brown hair, large, intelligent, light-brown eyes, and a shy smile that formed easily. Her buckskin clothing could not hide a slim, willowy figure that made her look tall. He never expected to find such an attractive woman out here in the wilderness!

When they had finished talking, the man got up and left. The woman smiled apologetically, "He will give you his answer when he has considered it." She turned to go.

Tom reached over and touched her arm. "I am going to have to talk to Indian people every day. Could you come up here to help me talk to them?"

"Yes, if it is agreeable to my father."

"What do they call you?"

"In your language, Gray Dove. My father says like the gentle bird."

"What was your White name?"

"It was Ruth Madison. That sounds so strange now. I haven't heard it for so long."

She smiled, and followed her father. Tom couldn't help thinking things were looking better, a lot!

That night, pictures of crossing the river, facing Seth Bollinger, getting buildings built, a police force, and the beautiful interpreter, all tumbled around in his mind until he thought he'd go crazy. Sleep just wouldn't come.

The next morning he felt like his brain wouldn't work anymore. After he'd eaten, he went back to his wagon to get his mind in order for the day's activities.

CHAPTER FOUR

Ole and Bascomb came up after they had eaten. Ole sat down on the wagon tongue. "Vell, the supplies are covered. Vat's next?"

"We've got to have some meat to go with the other food. Why don't you pick up a couple of rifles, and as soon as Capture gets here, I'll have him pick out a hunter to take with you. We'll see if we can train a couple of them to do the hunting for us."

Just then Horse Capture and Gray Dove came walking in with five Indians. Gray Dove smiled. "My father said, 'You are a wise man. You helped my wife on the trip over, and I will help you.'"

"Maple Leaf is his wife, and your mother?"

"Yes, she is my Indian mother. My birth mother died when I was sixteen."

"Maple Leaf is a great lady. I like her very much."

"My father says these are the carpenters. They will do as the soldier instructs them."

Tom turned to Bascomb. "Sergeant, find Thoreson and bring him here, then have him dig out a couple of axes, one for him and one for one other man. We had better not give them all axes at this point until they've settled into a routine. They probably still don't have very good feelings toward us." Bascomb left for the fires.

Tom turned back to Gray Dove. "Ask your father to select a married man to go with Sergeant Swensen to hunt for some meat for all of us. He will go back to the fires with him."

"Why a married man?"

"He will have more of an interest in getting food for his family." And, Tom thought to himself, not so anxious to turn on the soldier with his rifle.

Tom next went up to the bench where he wanted to put the warehouse and later the Tribal building, and eventually the Agency headquarters. He selected the locations for all three buildings and returned to his wagon.

When he got back, three Indians, Bascomb and Thoreson were waiting.

Tom said, "Thoreson, here is your crew. They have been instructed to follow your orders. None of them speak English so you'll have to use sign language. If you have a problem, come back and we'll straighten it out."

Gray Dove had been waiting nearby until he got through. "Do you want the agriculture and livestock men now?"

Tom looked at Bascomb. "Have you got the soldier leaders picked out for them?"

"Yes, Sir. Riley will push the cows, and Anderson will plow the gardens."

"Good. Gray Dove, tell your father we are ready. Sergeant, go with her to the fires, and get your soldiers acquainted with the men he picks. Gray Dove will introduce them. Then come back here and bring Anderson and his men. Have Riley come up after he has learned who his men are."

Everyone left and Tom said to himself, "All right, everyone is lined out but the police now, and Bascomb is taking care of that."

He sat down on the wagon tongue, and drew a long breath. Whew! Everything had to be done at once. He sat back against the bed of the wagon and closed his eyes for a few minutes. It was good to relax for just a bit.

He opened his eyes to see Gray Dove coming across the compound toward him. She was as graceful as a deer, and pretty, too! "The men will be here shortly. What would you like for me to do now?"

"Let's just wait a little until I get them on their way. Have a seat here on the wagon tongue."

She sat down beside him, and he could feel her nearness. It was intoxicating.

"Gray Dove, how do the people feel about us? I can imagine that it isn't good, having been captured and then marched clear up here, and then held here. I'd like them to know that I am sorry for that. The army didn't know what else to do with them after they were captured and so many settlers were being killed that they had to do something. This seemed like the most humane thing to do."

"Some are very angry, some know that they have been beaten in war and have accepted their fate. I think most of them have come to accept you and your men. They all have been good to us since we left the fort. I think the people will come to realize that you have their best interests at heart. You should know that these people have not killed the settlers. It has been the band of Broken Nose."

"I've met Broken Nose. He's the one that made me use that cane."

"He is bad. We have had several battles with his men. They are raiders."

"I hope we can get our police department going before he comes this way. How was it being raised by the Indians? How did they treat you?"

39

"The women beat my mother at first, until Chief Capture took her as his wife. Then she was accepted by all. The children teased me some, but we soon became good friends. Our friendship lasts until this day."

"I'm very glad you're here. I would be having one heck of a time getting all this across, if we couldn't communicate. Are there any others that speak English?"

"My friend, Pretty Rose. She speaks some English. I've tried to teach her."

Tom could see Anderson and his crew coming toward them and he stood, waiting. "Are you ready to go to work?"

Anderson grinned. "Lieutenant, my sign language is pretty rusty, but we'll give it our best try."

"Fine." Tom pointed to the flats below them. "We're going to build a barn on the far edge of the flat down there. We need to build a corral of about five acres that will butt up against it. Go to the supplies over there and pick out two axes. Give one to one of the Indians, and you take the other. Cut poles and stack them staggered, laying the end of one pole over the one next to it until you get them up about five feet high. You've seen pole fences. You and your axe man cut down the poles, and have the rest of them drag them to the fence line. Show them how to stack the poles. Go now, and good luck. Bring the axes back here at the end of every day."

The next few days kept Tom busy checking from one project to the next one. Bascomb had the tribal police patrolling with the soldiers, Thoreson had two men with axes now besides himself and was pulling the logs from the cut trees to the site with the wagon horses. Anderson had the corral nearly built, and had included a small creek in it to water the stock. In fact, some volunteer Indians were helping with building the corral project.

It was going too good. He had a feeling of some problem hiding in the background. He walked down to the fires where Gray Dove was sitting talking to her mother. When she saw him she got up and walked to meet him. "Did you want me?"

"Yes. Would your mother oversee the cooking chores? If the Indian women would be willing to do that, it could free up a couple more soldiers for other duty. Also, I need to ask you, can you write English?"

"Yes, my mother taught me that, also."

"Good. We need to get the names of every man, woman and child in the camp. Would you be willing to take on that job?"

"Yes, and I'll ask my mother if she will take the cooking job. I think she will. Everyone is getting pretty bored just sitting around. The ones that are working are the happiest."

She walked back and discussed it with her mother for some time, then came back to where Tom was standing. "My mother says she will take over the cooking. She has a lot of friends that will work with her."

The next week was taken up with solving problems of getting latrines dug for three hundred and fifty Indians, and his troops, settling disputes over food distribution, sleeping accommodations, where to get water, where to bathe, and a multitude of other minor problems that continued to crop up. Tom began to think he should have been a lawyer or a judge or something else than a soldier.

One morning after his crews had been working for better than a week, Tom asked Bascomb to have all his crew leaders meet with him before going to their work assignments.

When they arrived, Tom handed each of them a cup of coffee. "Gentleman, pull up a sack of grain. Sergeant, how are you coming with the tribal police?"

"They're coming along fine. I issued them some billed caps from the supplies as uniforms, and they are pleased with the respect they are being shown by the people, having been chosen as policemen. They are getting to be proud of what they are doing."

"Good. Thoreson, how is the building program going?"

"It started off a little rocky. The men didn't have any idea what to do, and were pretty reluctant to do anything, but once we got it going, they kinda took hold, and are working pretty well now. We still have a language problem, but we're getting through it."

"Riley?"

"We had the same problem to start with, but once they got the idea of how to lay the poles, they worked so hard that I had to give one more man an axe to keep poles out in front of the draggers. Now, we even have volunteers who were tired of layin' around the fires, and came down to help build the corrals."

"You men are doing a terrific job. Keep up the good work, and maybe we will get on top of this thing one of these days. I'm proud of you."

Tom dismissed them, and walked down to the fires to check on things. All seemed peaceful there. At least some things were starting to work.

Tom walked back to his wagon, broke out some pencils and paper and set them aside for Gray Dove, then, he walked down to where the horses were grazing, caught up Dusty and saddled him. He was getting cabin fever, also, and needed to get out in the open country and clear his brain a little.

He started west and rode to the reservation boundary, then turned south. The west boundary edged the desert, with the mountains to his left. He skirted the desert until he reached what he thought would be the south boundary, and climbed the mountains east of him until he reached the summit. He could see vast prairie lands below the mountains that stretched to the east boundary of his new reservation.

There was much in favor of this place for the Indians to be pleased with. They had mountains providing many small streams, long mile-wide meadows that could grow crops siding these streams, prairie lands stretching for miles to support cattle, and timber to meet their wood and building needs for a long time to come.

It was starting to get late, and Tom pointed Dusty back toward the camp.

Horse Capture and Gray Dove were waiting by his wagon when he got back. He put Dusty down with the other horses and hobbled him, then walked back to the wagon.

Gray Dove looked very worried. "One of the little boys died this afternoon. Many are saying it was because of the long march."

"I know the march was hard on many of the people. I wish there were something I could have done. Will you take me to the parents? I want to tell them how sorry I am."

"Yes, I'll take you, but first there is something my father wants to talk to you about. He says it is our custom to take the dead to the sacred burial ground, erect pole structures so they are near the heavens, and bid our goodbyes there."

"Tell him that I rode to the south boundary today, and I saw a place that might meet your needs. It is on the high mountain to the south, with crags reaching toward the sky. I believe it is in a location that would not be bothered by anyone traveling through. I will ride up there with him tomorrow, if he would like."

Gray Dove talked to her father for a time. Tom could tell she was trying to pass on the description he had given her. Then she turned back to Tom. "He said yes, and to thank you. I will take you to the parents now if you are ready."

The little boy was laid out on a blanket near one of the fires. Indians were standing all around him. Tom worked his way in to where the parents were. The mother was sitting on the ground near the boy, wailing, and the father was standing, staring straight ahead. Neither gave an indication that Tom was there. He knelt in front of the mother and put his hand on her shoulder. He tried to tell her how sorry he was.

She stopped for a while, looking at him, and gave him a sort of forced smile. Tom patted her shoulder, and then stood and shook hands with the father. The father looked down, and then into Tom's eyes, but Tom couldn't read anything from his gaze. He just stared straight into Tom's eyes. Tom left and returned to his wagon.

The next morning, Tom went to the pasture and brought Dusty and another horse up to the wagon and saddled them. Horse Capture was there shortly after that. They climbed into the saddles immediately and started south toward the mountains. There was no conversation between the two men on the climb.

Toward noon, Tom stopped at a small creek near the top, watered Dusty, and took a drink himself. The chief did the same. Then Tom took a package from his saddle bag and pulled out several strips of jerky. He handed half of them to Capture.

They ate in silence. Then Tom climbed back into the saddle and led the way on up the mountain, until they had to stop to walk the rest of the way. It was too steep and rocky to ride any further.

When they got to the top of the mountain, there was a flat, somewhat rocky area, possibly a half-mile across both ways. It was surrounded by rocky uplifts that were reduced to spires at their tops. It was almost like the shape of a crown, with small points sticking up all around the perimeter. From the edge of the area, the desert could be seen far below on the west side, the mountain range was to the north and toward the encampment. The grass prairie land extended to the east as far as the eye could see, and to the south was more desert, far below, that also ran to the horizon. It seemed to Tom that they were so high that they were half-way to Heaven to start with.

Tom stood silently while the chief took it in. The man stood for some time looking intently one way, then turning a little and looking some more, until he had taken in every side of the plot. Then he turned to Tom. There were tears in his eyes as he held out his hand and shook Tom's. Tom could tell the man was deeply moved.

They walked back down the mountain to the horses and rode back to camp.

Gray Dove made her usual trip to Tom's wagon after everyone had eaten. "My father asked me to thank you for finding the burial ground. He is very pleased with it. He will be up here presently. He has some things he wants to discuss with you."

"I know the boy's parents hate me with a passion. I can't blame them. They think the march was responsible for his death. They may be right - I don't know. I tried to go slow so they could keep up, but I wish that they knew I had no choice but to make them go."

"I know that, and I have tried to explain to them and others what your situation is. Some understand."

"Gray Dove, you are a jewel. I don't know what I would have done if not for you. You've made life a lot easier for me."

She smiled at him. "I'm glad."

He wanted to take her in his arms right there, and stood for a minute looking into her face. Then a sound behind him made him turn around. Chief Capture was standing there.

Tom made a gesture to the man to take a seat on the wagon tongue. He was going to have to get one of the woodsmen to make some real seats here one of these days.

Capture talked to his daughter for several minutes, then, she turned to Tom. "My father wants to thank you again for setting aside a burial ground for us."

"Tell him he is more than welcome."

Some further discussion went on between Gray Dove and her father. When they had finished, she sat looking at Tom, trying to form her words. "My father would like to have the burial ceremony for Indians only. He said the Indians would resent any of the whites being there. They have very recently been our enemies."

Tom got up and walked over to the old chief, leaned down and looked him in the eye. "Tell your father that I believe him to be an honorable man, that I can trust his word. If he will tell me that none of the Indians will try to escape, I will hold the soldiers here in camp while he is burying the boy."

Gray Dove again talked to her father at length. When she had finished, the chief turned around and walked back to the fires. She said, "He will talk to the others and get word back to you."

"When will the funeral be?"

"It's our custom to wait three suns—excuse me, three days, to allow for mourning."

"How are you coming on the list of names of all of the people?"

"I have the names of those at the first fire."

"Good. Why don't you go ahead with that today, or until your father wants to talk about the burial some more. I'll see what's happening with the other projects."

Tom walked up to the bench where the warehouse was under construction. The walls were up, doors and windows cut out, and Thoreson was astraddle a wall with a pole rafter in his hands, trying to wrestle it into place. He was cussing a blue streak, and his crew of Indians was standing around watching him. He looked down and saw Tom standing there. He started to rise up.

"I'm sorry, Lieutenant, I didn't see you there."

"At ease, Thoreson, don't stand on ceremony on the job. What's the problem?"

"I'm trying to get these long rafters in place and I can't be on both ends of it at once. I can't get them to understand what I want."

Tom crawled up the ladder to the log Thoreson was working on. "Here, show me what you want on this end and you go ahead on up to the center pole. Maybe if we get one in place, they can see how it's done."

They soon had the first rafter in place, and Thoreson showed his workers what he needed. Thoreson motioned for one of the workers to come up and he showed him what he wanted him to do.

Tom watched while they handed the next rafter up and it was soon in place, as well. It wouldn't be long until that building was finished and they could get the supplies inside.

Tom walked back down to the Indian camp site. He went over to fire number two and when he saw Gray Dove, he approached where she was taking down names. "Did you say there was someone else who could speak English?"

"Yes, my friend. I taught her. Her English isn't the best, but she can communicate."

"Would you ask her if she would be willing to go up to the warehouse, and stay with them to act as a go-between. Thoreson is having trouble getting his men to understand what he needs done. And it will get a lot more complicated from now on."

"I'm sure she will, I'll ask her to go up there."

Tom smiled. "Thanks, Gray Dove. Like I said, you're a jewel."

He left the fire and walked down to the corral. It was finished, and Angus and his crew were busy packing rocks up to the barn site for its foundation.

He hung his jacket on a limb, and helped the crew pack rocks until noon when they all walked back up to the fires to eat. Maple Leaf and her crew had been making tasty meals with what they had to work with.

That afternoon, he was glad to get back to his work at the wagon. About the middle of the afternoon, Ole and his helper came in with a couple of deer. When it was butchered out and the meat taken to the cooks, Ole came up to the wagon.

"Ay heard about the boy, Tom. Ay'm sorry. You didn't need any more complications."

"I think we've about got it worked out. They are going to bury him day after tomorrow. I've agreed with the chief, if he will guarantee that no one will leave, they can go to the burial ground without us, to bury the boy."

"You can't yoost let them go by themsel'es. They'll be in Mexico by night! You have the large size rocks in your head!"

"I know it, Ole, but I trust that old man. I think he's as straight as that wagon tongue. I looked him in the eye and asked him for his word."

"You know your career is ower, if they skedaddle?"

"Yeah, I know. I just think he will do the right thing."

"Vell, partner, Ay t'ink you yoost better hope that man up above looks down on you vith favor. Ay vish you luck!"

Later in the afternoon, Gray Dove and the chief came to the wagon. Tom offered them a seat on the wagon tongue, but the chief wanted to stand.

Dawn said, "My father says that you have his word, and that of the others, that no one will leave. They will come back here when the burial is over."

Tom stuck out his hand. "Then it's agreed, Chief. The soldiers will remain here until your return." They shook hands.

The next morning when the noncoms got to the wagon, Tom was feeling drug out from another mostly sleepless night. Ole pointed to him. "It's not likker, it's yoost layin' avake dreaming about some voman, or somet'ing. Ay t'ink ve should send him back to the fort, or somewhere, for a short rest."

"I think I'll take you down to the creek for a recharge on that water-soaked brain, Ole."

Addressing the group, Tom said, "Tomorrow morning after all have eaten, the Indians are going to make a march up the mountains for a burial of that boy that died. I want all the soldiers to form two lines along the trail leaving the camp site that the Indians can march between. Stand at attention with your rifles raised up in front of you. Bascomb, why don't you have the tribal police form two lines just beyond yours. It will give them a sense of belonging to the police department, and give them some prestige among the other Indians."

Bascomb stared at Tom. "Begging your pardon, Sir, but you aren't letting them go by themselves, are you? It'll be the last we see of them!"

"You may be right, Sergeant, but I have the Chief's word, and somehow I trust him. I may live to regret it, but there is going to come a time when we have to put some trust in their leaders, and I am going to start now with him."

"Yes, Sir. We'll be ready."

The next morning after everyone had eaten, Gray Dove came up to the wagon. "They're ready to go."

"All right. Would you give us a few minutes before you leave?"

Tom walked over to where the soldiers were standing. "All right, men, a column of twos. When we get past the fires, drop to the side, stand facing each other across the trail with your rifles vertical in front of you. They will walk down the trail between you. Are you ready, Sergeant?"

"Yes, Sir."

"All right. March them out."

The soldiers marched out past the fires and the Indian people standing there watching. The tribal policemen fell in behind the soldiers and formed two lines just beyond the soldiers. They were packing rifles. Bascomb must have issued them rifles for the occasion!

Tom was proud of them. They carried it off just as he wanted, to impress the Indians that their burial ceremony was a sacred thing to them, as well, and that they were honoring the young boy.

Tom walked over to the chief. "Chief, I will walk with you down past the soldiers, and we'll leave you there."

Gray Dove translated, and the chief nodded. Tom and the chief started from the fires and all of the Indians fell in behind. Four Indian men carried a stretcher with the body of the boy on it. When they reached the last tribal policeman, Tom stepped to the side of the trail beside him, unsheathed his sword and held it in a vertical position in front of him as the Indians walked by. The soldiers and tribal policemen stood in formation until the Indians reached the timber and disappeared, then, they marched back to the fires and were dismissed.

Tom walked back to the fires. It all seemed so empty with the Indians gone. The soldiers went back to their usual tasks. Thoreson was back up on the tribal building he was starting to build. Anderson was back down on the barn, and Bascomb was taking the tribal police out in back for a lesson in handling the army rifles. Ole went out alone to find some game.

Tom went down to the pasture and found Dusty. He brought him back up and saddled him. He hadn't been out to the eastern part of the reservation yet. This might be a good time.

Before long, he was riding through a mile-wide valley, with a stream winding down through the middle. The soil was dark and friable where it was exposed. This should be an ideal place to start the farms. They could set out twenty acres in each plot with access to the creek. That should be enough acreage to provide a living for a family. He'd have to tell Riley to ride out and look it over.

As Tom rode, the country opened up, and wide expanses were covered with prairie grass. All of this land would support a great herd. The tribe could have all the beef it needed for the people all the time. They wouldn't have to depend on the army to supply their meat needs. He was elated.

Continuing to the eastern boundary, he found that the vegetation remained the same. He rode back to the camp as the rays of the sun were getting longer. Things were starting to shape up.

As he topped the ridge and looked down into the camp site, he could see a dust cloud rising from the pasture. He hurried down, and could see a herd of cattle milling around within the enclosure. He kicked Dusty into a trot and rode up to his wagon. A group of men were seated there, drinking coffee in front of one of the fires. They were dressed as cattlemen.

Tom ground-reined Dusty and strode over to the fire. A soldier rose from the rock he was sitting on and walked over to Tom. "Are you Lieutenant Colter?"

"Yes, I am."

"Master Sergeant Harry Fister, Lieutenant. I'm the quartermaster from the fort. I'm delivering this herd of cattle. There are also six wagons that should be here tomorrow, loaded with supplies. Where are your Indians?"

"They are having a burial today for a young boy. They are all attending the funeral."

"I see quite a few soldiers here. Aren't you guarding the Indians?"

"No. You can tell Colonel Brewster we have satisfied Indians on this reservation." Tom had his fingers crossed behind his back.

"You have the only Indians in the United States that way then, if that's true."

Tom decided that he should change the subject if he could. "When your wagons come, take them up to that building you see over there on the bench. That's our warehouse. Unload them in it."

"You already have a warehouse? I thought you just got here!"

"We've been here over a month now."

After they had eaten the evening meal, Tom and the quartermaster sat talking to the cattlemen over a cup of coffee. Tom asked them about where they headquartered.

"We're with the Bar C out of Nebraska."

"You agreed to bring the cattle here as part of the selling price?

"That's right."

"Would you do it again for the same price?"

"I reckon."

"How long did it take you to make the drive?"

"'Bout a month."

"That's good to know."

Tom stood. "I'm about tuckered out. I think I'll hit the soogans. Fister, what time do you think the wagons will get here?"

"They weren't too far behind us. I'd say before noon. Say, I still don't see any Indians."

"They'll be here."

Tom went to his wagon, and crawled into his soogans. Ole was asleep when he got there, but woke up as Tom crawled in. "Long day?"

"Yeah, I rode over to the east boundary. There's a lot of good grazing over there. We could run a lot of cattle."

"You seen the chief yet?"

"Not yet. He'll be here," and said to himself, "I hope."

"Vell, ven they let you out of yail, you can alvays go to cowboying. You said you vould like that."

"Before that happens, I'm going to fill one big Swede's mouth with lye soap. He's always talking too much."

The wagons rolled in the next day just before noon. Master Sergeant Fister directed them to the warehouse, and they started unloading right after the noon meal. Tom watched the unloading. When it was done, he pointed to the stack of material brought in.

"Sergeant, there are only three stoves in that bunch, I counted fifty cots, and it looked like maybe one hundred blankets. I have three hundred and fifty Indians sleeping out there by the fires. About two-thirds of them are women and kids. Tell me how I'm going to keep them out of the weather and warm with that? Winter will be coming on soon, and those kids will be sleeping in the snow."

"Lieutenant, I can only tell you, this is what I was ordered to bring. Besides that, I don't think you have any Indians. I think they're all sleeping in Mexico."

"That's my concern, Sergeant. I'm going to prepare a letter to Colonel Brewster for you to take back to him. I have got to have another three hundred cots, and blankets to go with them before winter sets in. I also need three more large stoves, and by next spring, I will need about one hundred small cooking stoves. I know that funding is a problem, but it's a problem what to do with this many Indians, too, and that is an immediate problem. When are you leaving?"

"Just as soon as I can get my crew together."

"Stop by my wagon before you go and I'll have the letter ready."

The letter was hardly finished when Fister came by the wagon. "Is there anything else you want sent back to Brewster?"

"Just tell him that we are here, and that so far, everything is proceeding as planned."

"Does that include losing three hundred and fifty Indians?"

"No, and I don't appreciate the implication. We haven't lost any Indians. Give my regards to the Colonel."

Fister saluted, turned on his heel and went back to his crew. Tom walked over to where the cattlemen were mounting their horses. He thanked them for bringing the cattle and wished them a safe journey back, then stood and watched the wagons until they were out of sight.

Returning to the fire, he poured himself a cup of coffee, and sat down on the wagon tongue. It was getting to be another day, and still no Indians. Were all of the naysayers right? Had he been a damned fool for trusting the chief? There was no question he could be stripped of his commission, thrown out of the army, and maybe even sent to jail if they didn't return. He had been so sure the old chief could be trusted. He was sure that they were all tired yet from the march coming here; he wouldn't think they'd be ready for another long walk. The coffee suddenly tasted sour. He threw it out on the ground.

Tom walked to the edge of the wagon bench. He could hear Anderson pounding on his barn on the bench below.

Sounds of shots came from the edge of the woods across the meadow. Bascomb was teaching his men how to shoot the army rifles. He really was doing a job with the Indian police. He had them marching, making the rounds with his soldiers, and had them dressed in the visored caps. They had seemed really proud of that when they lined up to let the Indians walk between them.

The pounding noise from the tribal building stopped. Thoreson had been working on it. Tom decided to walk up there. There was nothing to do where he was.

Thoreson was digging off to the side of the new building. What could that be for? Tom walked over to the spot.

"Thoreson, what are you doing?"

"Building a saw-pit, Sir."

"What is a saw-pit?"

"Well, you lay a log across the pit, and cut square boards out of the logs. I saw it when I was stationed in the South. We'll put a platform at the edge of the pit for one man to stand on, and the other will get down in the pit, and they'll saw the log lengthwise, just wide enough to make a board. I saw two crosscut saws in the warehouse and it gave me the idea. I was wondering how I was going to make floors for the buildings."

"Is there another shovel in the warehouse?"

"Yeah, over on the left side."

"Hang on. I'll give you a hand."

Tom went to the warehouse and picked up a shovel and started digging on the other end of the pit. It felt good to do some physical work. It gave him something else to think about besides whether the Indians were going to come back or not. They worked until dark, and Tom was glad to get something to eat at the fire, and then hit the soogans.

The morning fire cast a flickering light on the tarp cover as Tom came over for breakfast. He picked up a cup and poured himself some coffee, and the cook soon had some bacon and hotcakes ready. Tom sat on a nearby rock and wondered about his Indians as he ate.

When he had finished, he put his plate into the dishwater tub and thought he'd be glad when Maple Leaf got back. The troopers' cooking was not quite the same.

Sergeant Bascomb came up and filled his plate, then sat on the ground next to Tom. "No Indians yet, Sir?"

"None yet, Sergeant. We'll give them until noon, and if they haven't arrived by then, we'd better go investigate. I hate to do it because I was wanting to impress the chief that I trusted him implicitly. It might make it easier to have him do things for us if he thought we trusted him. Anyway, have a couple of your best men ready to go after lunch."

CHAPTER FIVE

· The rays of the sun were cutting a colorful design in the fluffy clouds above his head as the old chief settled down against a rock by the fire. Gray Dove came over and sat beside him. "You are tired, Father. You should have left the work for the younger men."

"A man can't lead from behind the bush, Daughter. When I am no longer able to stay with the men, I'll let some younger man be the chief. I am tired, but I believe they are, as well. We have our burial ground ready. We will go back to the camp in the morning."

"I'll fetch you some food."

She went to her food sack and brought out some jerked venison that she had prepared when the hunters brought in the first deer. She got a few sticks for herself, also, and sat beside him, leaning against the other side of the rock.

"Daughter, I have something to discuss with you. I have seen how you look at that white man. You have spent nearly all of your time with him since we arrived at the camp. He is of your color, and that may make him attractive to you, but he is a soldier. He has fought our people, which makes him an enemy. He forced our people across miles of rough country. How can you look on him with favor?"

"Father, I believe that he is a good man. I know how hard he works to look after our people. Look how he brought Mother up to his wagon when she got too tired to walk. He has his soldiers working to build buildings for us. His chief has told him to bring us to the camp, and he is trying to make things as good for us as he can. He could have sent the soldiers to guard us up here at the burial ground, but he didn't want to intrude on our ceremonies, and took your word that you would bring all the Indians back. He is our friend."

"What you say is true, Daughter, and I should withhold judgment for a time. I just don't want you to be enamored by his uniform or good looks, and then live a life that is foreign to you and bring you unhappiness the rest of your life. I did give him my word that I would bring all of the Indians back, and I intend to keep that word."

Two young warriors came up to where they were sitting. The tallest one spoke first. "Chief Capture, are you going back to the camp?"

"Yes, I gave my word to the Lieutenant that we would all return. He kept his word and kept the soldiers from our ceremony here, and I will keep my word that we will come back."

"You can't trust a white-eyes. They murder our people, hold us in prison, and then make us sleep in the dirt in that camp. We are going south."

"It is true that they have killed many of our people, as our people have killed many of theirs. The truth is that we were defeated in a war. They have decided that they need to keep us on reservations to protect their people. As a defeated people, we have little choice but to work with them. Where would you go if you went south?"

"We will find Broken Nose. He is leading a group of warriors, and we will defeat the white-eyes."

"Broken Nose is an outlaw. He may kill a few white-eyes, but in the end, he will die. There are too many of them for us to fight and win. You would lose your life, also, if you joined him."

"Huh! You are an old man, and have lost your will to be a warrior. We will go, and count many coups."

"No, I have given my word as a chief of the Sioux. We will all return. You will not bring dishonor to our people."

The two young men left the fire, talking to each other. Horse Capture sat watching them, and wondering if they would obey, or if they would go on their own and leave the group. It was harder and harder to get compliance from the younger ones who felt the need for fighting. They did not have the benefit of the experience of their elders. It was always so.

Gray Dove soon left her father and walked over to where her mother was bedded down for the night. She lay down beside her.

"Mother, I believe I am in love with the Lieutenant. Father thinks it is wrong. How do you feel about it if I were to marry him?"

"Daughter, I raised you to think for yourself. Listen to what your heart tells you. I rode beside him for days in that wagon. I think he has a good heart."

Gray Dove lay there, thinking about the soldier. She wished that he would take her in his arms one of these days. She wasn't sure that he felt anything toward her, though, except to translate for him. Maybe he couldn't stand the fact that she was raised by the Indians. How could she find out? At least she could lie here and think about him. They couldn't stop her from doing that. She lay there waiting for sleep, with a smile on her face.

CHAPTER SIX

Dust boiled up from the wagon wheels as they clattered through the gates of the fort. Colonel Brewster rose from his chair and walked to the window to look out. It was the wagons he had sent to Colter with the supplies. They had made good time.

He looked over to the General. "Well, George, we'll soon find out how our newest reservation is making out. The supply wagons just pulled in."

"I'll be anxious to hear. I still think you'd have been better off giving a regular officer that duty than to a scout. They are notoriously unmilitary, and independent."

"I've ridden with Colter many times, and he is a man I'd trust my life to. He is smart and he knows Indians, probably better than any man in my command. It's going to be a big job putting a reservation together from scratch. I have every confidence in him."

The orderly knocked and entered the room. "Master Sergeant Fister to see you, Sir."

"Send him in."

"Master Sergeant Fister reporting, Sir."

"Sergeant, this is General Hadley. What did you find at the reservation? Are they coming along?"

"They have a warehouse nearly done to store the food and supplies, and a tribal building started. The corral is built, and a barn partially built. That is about the extent of the improvements."

"That's pretty good for the short time they've been there. What is the condition of the Indians?"

"That's just it, Sir. There are no Indians."

"What do you mean, 'No Indians'?"

"I was told they were somewhere in the mountains at a burial service for some young boy. The trouble is all of the soldiers were there at the camp working on buildings or other jobs."

"You can't be serious! No one was guarding the Indians?"

"No, Sir."

The General jumped to his feet. "I told you, Brewster. You can't depend on a scout! Now all the lives lost in capturing those heathens will be for naught, and we will have to go fight them again. I demand that you call a court martial for that scout immediately. He should be thrown in irons!"

"I'll look into it, and see what the story is. This doesn't sound like Colter at all."

"No, I don't want any friendship you have for this man coloring the proceedings. You're to hold a court martial, and I want the results sent to me as soon as it's over."

"Yes, Sir, General. Sergeant, did you have anything else?"

"Sir, here is a list of supplies that Lieutenant Colter sent. He said he desperately needed them before cold weather set in."

"The General harumphed. "Why does he need supplies if there are no Indians there?"

Brewster said: "Very well, Sergeant. Thank you for the report. You are dismissed."

The General looked over as Brewster started pacing the floor. "Well, what are you going to do with your scout, Brewster? The dumbest recruit wouldn't let that bunch run free. I've never thought scouts had the brains to get in out of the rain. They just run wild and some officers think they are smart. This offense has to be answered and I want you to convene a court martial as soon as possible, and I will be waiting for a report."

"Yes, Sir, but it may take some time. We have a logistics problem. He is way over there, and we have to arrange for someone to take his place before we can even send for him."

"Well, do it as fast as you can. That really burns me that someone would be so reckless as to let three hundred and fifty Indians go free without even chasing them. The man is a disgrace to the uniform. I'll be leaving in the morning, but send a dispatch after the court convenes."

After the general had left the room, Brewster resumed his pacing. What has happened? Colter wasn't a ne'er-do-well. He was a smart, dependable soldier. There was something here that didn't meet the eye. He didn't have a choice, though. He had to have a court martial hearing. First, he had better get Fister on finding the supplies that Colter asked for. They were things the Indians needed whether Tom survived the court martial, or not. How did things like this happen?

CHAPTER SEVEN

Fog rolled down over the cliffs above the hidden enclave that he had used since the outbreak of the war. Soldiers had chased him many times, but taking to the stream and riding in it until he came to the malpais, and then following it up into the mountains, he had reached a breach in the cliffs. This led to a large hollow in the mountain, giving him a perfect hideaway. They had never followed beyond searching the banks of the stream for tracks.

Broken Nose looked at his warriors lounging around the camp. They were top fighting men. He could be riding onto a white man's farm, kill the residents, burn the buildings, and be gone before anyone knew of it. Even the smaller white villages were not able to stop them. He was just as great as Naiche or Geronimo, or any of them. One day he would be known among all tribes as the greatest warrior of all.

It had been a moon since their last raid. It was time to make another run. He was still smarting from the defeat when they had attacked the soldiers. He would rescue the Indians at the reservation; that would make him great in their eyes. Horse Capture would have to admit then that he, Broken Nose, should be chief of all the Sioux. He had had only a small raiding party that time. Now, he would have his whole band of warriors. There were very few soldiers, and the braves there now could help him. It would be an easy victory!

Broken Nose looked over to where Otter was watching a stick game. He finally got his attention and waved him over. "It is time we made a raid. The braves are getting restless. I think we should go make a raid on the reservation."

"Chief, I think you had better think twice. I know you have a grudge against that pony soldier, but think what he and his men did to us when we tried to attack them. We lost over half our men, and barely got out ourselves."

Broken Nose grinned. "The last I saw of that pony soldier he had my spear running all the way through his leg. The next time it will be through his heart! My men are anxious to taste the white man's blood again."

"That may be, my Chief, but you must remember, even though they are full of energy and want so much to prove their worth as warriors, they don't have the experience that your old warriors did, and look what the white-eyes did to them. I think we should let them taste some easy blood first. There are some white-eyes' farms down in the valley that will be a lot easier targets. Let them breathe a little smoke like that first, and then take on the pony soldiers."

Broken Nose sat looking into his fire, and thinking of Otter's words. Finally, he looked up at Otter and slapped him on the shoulder. "My friend, I have listened to your words of wisdom, and I believe you are right. First, you and I will plan our raid, and then we will call the warriors together and go burn some white-eyes' farms. Then I will go get that pony soldier and his men. I will show that Horse Capture what a great chief I have become!"

A light came on in the window of the house below the ridge where they had stopped, and shortly thereafter, a man left the building and walked to the barn, carrying a bucket.

Broken Nose waved his men in closer and when they were in place, he let out an ear-splitting war cry and raced toward the barn. The man ran back toward the house, but before he was half way to the building, he fell, a quill of arrows sticking out of his back. The warriors ran into the house, killing and scalping all of the occupants, a woman and three children, and then set fire to the buildings.

Broken Nose led the party riding in a circle around the burning buildings, chanting their victory cry. Some of the Indians waved bits of clothing, and other articles, they had picked up while they were inside.

After they had tired of this, and the buildings were nothing more than a pile of ashes, Broken Nose waved them on toward the next farm.

They had ridden about a half hour before the next homestead came into view. The farmhouse and barn were made of logs. There were two smaller sheds and a corral. Broken Nose sent two of his braves to catch up the horses in the corral and take them away. When that was done, he once again had the Indians surround the homestead and wait for his signal. Once more they would count coup which he could shake in the great Chief Capture's face.

Their war-cries resounded from the surrounding hills as his warriors once more charged into the yard of the white eyes. There was no sign of life from the buildings.

Broken Nose dismounted and signaled for his men to do the same. They crept silently toward the house. Broken Nose was coming up to the porch, ready to break out a window there, when blasts in every direction came from the building. Guns were spouting fire on all sides of the house.

Broken Nose felt an impact on his shoulder that knocked him to the ground. He quickly crawled around behind a bush. As he surveyed the yard, he could see several of his men lying there motionless. Another was just outside the yard fence, writhing and moaning.

Another barrage came from the house, and two more of his men fell to the ground. Broken Nose jumped to his feet and ran for his horse. He could hear the whistle of the bullets as they sailed by his ear. He yelled for his men to leave.

He rode to the ridge to the south of the homestead and stopped his pony there. His men came in, one by one. Some were wounded, all were somber. A few of the younger ones wanted to go back, but Broken Nose decided that this was the place the white- eyes had gathered for protection, or maybe it was a large family. There were too many guns there. He led his men back to his camp, a very dejected chief.

Once back at his camp, he built a fire for warmth, and sat staring into the dancing flames. Otter came over and sat beside him. Otter noticed Broken Nose's bleeding shoulder and rose to find a cloth to bind the wound.

"The first raid we took many coups, the second one we brought back four horses. It was not all bad."

Broken Nose felt his face turn red with shame. How could he have such bad luck? His braves were ready to fight. They were well-armed, and they should have had the element of surprise. The longer he thought about it, the angrier he became.

"I cannot delay longer. We will take one moon to train the young ones more, and then we will hit the reservation. If I wait too long, the soldier will be gone, and I will get him if it is with my dying breath."

Otter threw up his hands. "Your obsession with that soldier is going to be the death of you. He has as many soldiers as you have braves. He has guns while we have mostly bows and arrows and some have spears. You will lose many braves, and probably your own life."

"It is something I must do."

Broken Nose sat staring at the fire. Once more, he had been turned back by the whites. His hatred centered on the soldier at the reservation. He was the one that had started it. And Horse Capture! He thinks he is so great, and so wise! He, Broken Nose, will show them all!

CHAPTER EIGHT

A great bank of heavy clouds came up the valley in a tidal wave, then engulfed the camp and turned everything damp. Tom felt the moisture when he pulled his hand out of his blankets and let it rest on the ground. He crawled out and fed the banked-up fire. He filled the coffee pot from a canteen, added the coffee grounds, and set it on a rock against the fire.

Ole groaned, and sat up. "Some people sure make a lot of noise, yoost putting some coffee on the fire."

"Some people could get up and do it themselves, if it doesn't suit them."

"Yah, Ay didn't hear a t'ing."

"You hunting today?"

"Yah, Tom, Ay vould like to take two policemen with me today. Ay t'ink there is some buffalo yoost off the reserwation. Ay saw some sign the last time Ay vas down that vay."

"We're supposed to keep the Indians on the reservation. Don't you think that might give them license to go off by themselves later? Well, we need the meat. Go ahead and do it."

"Yah, Ay vill see if Bascomb can lend me another soldier. Ve need to start bringing in enough meat so they can start making their pemmican and yerky for vinter."

When they had finished eating, Ole went after his horses, and Tom went down to the big fire to find Bascomb. Sergeant Bascomb had his crew of soldiers in front of him when Tom arrived. Tom looked at the group.

"Sergeant, Swensen needs an extra soldier today to help with the hunt. Can you spare one?"

"Yes, Sir."

"Good, and when you're through here, send Anderson, Riley, and Thoreson up to my wagon before they start the day."

When the trio arrived at his wagon, Tom offered them all a cup of coffee. "Sit down, men, we need to have a talk. Thoreson, how are you coming on the tribal building?"

"The logs are all cut and hauled in to the site. Rafters are cut, and I'll have the cover ready today. All I need is my crew to put it together."

"Riley?"

"The exterior of the barn is done. We were putting up the stanchions when the Indians left. I've been cutting some logs for interior walls since then."

"When they get back, I want you to stop on the barn for now. You can finish that later. Right now, we need to get a fairly good-sized smokehouse built to start smoking a big supply of jerky. Swensen is going to try to find some buffalo for smoking."

"Anderson?"

"We have one cabin finished and one plot fenced. I have enough logs cut for the next cabin as soon as my crew returns. When will they be back, Lieutenant?"

"They should be back today. I haven't heard from them since they left."

"You don't think they flew the coop, do you?"

"No. They'll be back." Tom wished that he felt as confident as he tried to sound. "All right, let's get on with it. One more thing, you all will be leaving in another five months, or so, going back to the fort. I want you to observe your crew of Indians and pick out a leader. Let him take a little responsibility now and then to develop him as the leader of the group, and for the men to accept him as the leader."

Tom sat watching the men leave and go to their job sites. What was happening with Horse Capture? He could have sworn that the old chief would be back with the Indians. Ole was right. If they did try to leave, it would be the end of his career. It might even be a jail sentence. Brewster had trusted him to take care of this bunch of Indians, and to keep them on the new reservation, and it was starting to look like he had done neither one.

As the day wore on, Tom grew more and more nervous about the lack of Indians. Why had he been so foolish as to trust the old chief? He was so sure he could! Well, he'd give it the rest of the day. Tonight he'd have Bascomb ready the troops for a ride through the mountains tomorrow, find the Indians and bring them back. He just couldn't believe he was going to have to do that!

The clouds that had risen during the day were starting to settle back down toward the ground when Ole and the two soldiers came in with their horses loaded with meat. Tom went with them to the warehouse.

Ole shouldered a quarter of meat and laid it on a blanket. "Ve have the meat. Do you have the Indians to eat it?"

"Not so's you'd notice it. Did you find a big herd?"

"Sizeable. Ve'll go back tomorrow. They didn't get too spooked of our shooting and maybe they vill stick around until then."

"Riley started on a smokehouse today. As soon as that's done, we'll get the meat in there."

Tom heard a commotion and turned around. Coming down the trail was Horse Capture and his Indians! Tom felt like he could kiss that old chief right there. He hurried back down to the fires to greet him."

Horse Capture was just lowering himself to the ground when Tom arrived. He walked over to the old chief.

"Hello, Chief. Did you have some trouble up there? I thought you would be back before this."

Gray Dove came over to where Tom was standing and gave him a big smile. She spoke to the old chief, then, turned to Tom. "My father said to tell you that he took time to make the burial ground suitable for future deaths. He is sorry if he caused you concern."

"He did not cause me concern. I had every faith that his word was good. I just knew you were without food, and that your water supplies might be getting low." He mentally crossed his fingers and hoped that a little white lie might not hurt.

Gray Dove related this to her father and they talked some more. "My father told me to tell you thanks."

"I'll leave you now to get settled, something to eat, and a rest. You will be up to the wagon in the morning?"

She smiled again. "Yes, I'll be there."

The sun was peeking over the mountains by the time Tom was through with the morning chores. He paced up and down in front of the wagon, waiting for Gray Dove to come up. He was anxious to see her. Seeing her briefly yesterday had made him realize how much his life had revolved around her lately. He enjoyed very much having her with him. He sat down by the fire and poured a cup of coffee.

He saw her coming up along the line of wagons. She was more beautiful every day. She walked with grace, and held her head up as if she was facing the world with courage, and enjoying life to the fullest. That was one of the things he liked about her. In spite of all the challenges she faced, it was always with a cheerful demeanor.

"Good morning, Gray Dove. A cup of coffee before we start?"

"Yes, please. I would like that."

Tom poured two cups of coffee and handed one to her. They walked back up to his wagon. He indicated a pile of blankets where she could sit, and lean back against the wagon wheel. "Tell me about your trip. Did you have any problems?"

"None that my father couldn't take care of. Five young men wanted to leave and go south, but my father insisted they stay, as he had given his word to you. They didn't like it, but they stayed."

"I can tell your father is well respected by all his people."

"The old ones, yes, but some of the younger ones think they know more than he does. I fear they will cause trouble."

"I hope we'll be able to handle it. Do most of the people hate us?"

"Some. Others know we were defeated in the war, and I think appreciate that you are trying to help them. My father has been telling them that you have been considerate of their needs as best you could under the circumstances."

"I appreciate that. Now, how are we doing on the names?"

"I have them all here on these papers. There are three hundred and forty two names."

"Good, that will help. As soon as we get the tribal building finished, I thought we would move the women and children in there. We will have a large heating stove in there to keep them warm. I'll try to arrange for the men to sleep in the warehouse and the barn until we can get better accommodations. At least they can get in out of the weather this way."

"The women have been tanning the hides of the animals the hunters have been bringing in. They have enough for three teepees ready to lace together."

"Good, tell your father to designate two other families to use them. I want him to keep one for himself and set it up next to the tribal building. That way, everyone will have a place to go to talk to him. It can be the official tribal office until we can get one built. Not only that, you will have a home again, which will make me happy."

"My father will not like going into a lodge when others have not."

"I know, but he needs to have a place where he can meet with his people in private. Away from me and from the other soldiers, and the other tribal members. They need to be able to speak freely to him. All right, now, how about you and I going over the list of people and identifying their families."

The list of people gradually was reduced to families. Tom couldn't help looking at Gray Dove as she had her head bent down over the list, trying to put families together from the list of names. She was lovely. He wanted to take her in his arms.

That evening when they had finished the list, and Gray Dove was making preparations to go back to her fire, Tom took her arm. "Gray Dove, would you walk down by the creek with me tonight? I just feel the need for some company."

She smiled. "I'd love that."

She felt like skipping all the way back to her fire. He had finally noticed she was a woman, and not just an interpreter!

The shadows cast by the sun's rays were getting longer, and the evening dusk was starting to settle in, when Tom arrived at Gray Dove's fire. She came over to meet him.

Tom said, "Before we leave, there is one thing I need to have you tell your father. Tell him to pick out a dozen or so women to pick camas roots tomorrow. I will send a soldier with them with a wagon. Also tell him to pick out seven men he can trust to hunt for game here on the reservation. I got to thinking about what you said about the hides for teepees. We can start making them faster and setting families up in them. We'll smoke the meat in the smokehouse and they can take grain from the warehouse, the meat, and the camas roots, and start making pemmican for this winter."

Gray Dove left and conferred with her father and soon returned. "My father says it will be done."

Tom took her hand and they left for the creek area. Suddenly, as they walked, the strain he had been under seemed to kind of wash away. The gurgle of the creek as it tumbled over the rocks, and the feel of Gray Dove's hand in his, all seemed to have a mesmerizing effect on him. He felt more at peace with the world.

After walking along the creek for a time, they came to a deep, green pool in the water. Tom saw a mossy spot under a pine tree just above the pool and led Gray Dove over to it. They sat staring at the water, not talking, each deeply engrossed in their own thoughts.

Tom put his arm around her waist. "Gray Dove, there's something----"

She put her finger on his lips to quiet him, and leaned over and kissed him. Tom responded, holding her close in his embrace and gently returning her kiss.

Finally, he released her. "Gray Dove, I have been wanting to do that forever. I just never had the nerve. I didn't mean to take advantage. I--."

She put her finger on his lips again. "Let's just leave it like it is, and enjoy the creek for now."

They sat and talked about their past lives that had led up to the present.

Tom asked, "Gray Dove, what do you remember about your early years?"

"My parents lived in a small prairie town in the Midwest. My father was a storekeeper. My mother was the schoolteacher. Someone talked to my father about going farther west and finding a big ranch. He got itchy feet, and decided that is what he wanted to do, although he had no idea what ranching was like.

"We packed up and moved west across the plains. He found a land office, filed on a homestead, and we moved out onto it and built a shack and a small barn. With the money he got from the store, he bought some farm equipment, a pair of mules, and supplies to last us a while. I was too young to remember much about that. I think I was about five.

"We struggled to make a living, but my father wasn't much of a farmer. He did make enough that we survived, and that was about it. Mother taught me schooling, and my brother, also, when he came along. The year I was ten, the settlers set up a school near us, and we went there.

"One day, soon after I was twelve, the Sioux made a raid in that part of the country. My father was killed and my mother, my brother and I were taken captive. They gave us to some Indian women, and they made slaves of us, making us do a lot of things they didn't want to do. Some of them would beat us with sticks if we weren't doing the work fast enough.

"One day, one of the women was beating my mother with a stick because she left some meat on one of the hides she was supposed to clean. Father came along and made her stop, and he took us into his teepee and kept my mother as a wife, and me as his daughter. I have lived well since then."

"Where is your brother?"

"I don't know. He had been taken with other boys to make warriors of them, and eventually was passed on to another Sioux tribe. I haven't seen or heard of him since."

"Maybe someday we can find him, somehow. Did you feel hatred for the Indians after they captured you?"

"I did at first, but as time went on and Father and Maple Leaf both treated us well, the hate began to subside. Soon after that, my mother became very ill and died. I made friends with some of the younger Indian girls, and we had fun playing. That helped, as well. What about you?"

"I was born on a farm in Kentucky. My folks raised cows, horses, chickens, hogs, and kids. There was an old neighbor that knew Daniel Boone. He taught me how to hunt, trap, and to get through the woods without making any noise while I was following a trail. There were also some friendly Indians and I played with them.

"My brothers were older than me and went into the army during the war. I was too young to go. I thought they were great heroes, and when I got old enough, I enlisted, too. When they found out I could follow a track, and that I had some experience with Indians, they made me a scout. That's all I did, until I met Broken Nose. You might say he made me an Indian Agent."

"Are you sorry?"

"Well, I didn't like getting wounded, but I did get to meet you. I think it was a good trade."

"Does your leg still hurt you?"

"No, I can hardly feel it now."

"I'm glad they made you the Indian Agent. I think our people will be very glad you are their agent, too, when they get over being captured and brought here. A few may not."

When it was time to head back to the fires, Tom helped her to her feet, put his arms around her, and kissed her tenderly. "Can we do this every night?"

She laughed at him. "Do you mean can you kiss me every night?"

"Tom turned red. "No, I meant could we walk down here every night?"

"That will depend on how busy the Indian Agent is."

Tom noticed the old chief watching them closely as they approached the fires. He took her hands in his. "I'll see you in the morning."

Walking back to his wagon, he felt like singing.

CHAPTER NINE

This branch of the Sioux did not have many fighting men, but he was able to persuade several to join him and the last warrior to come forward was a hulking, mean-looking man. Broken Nose walked around him. This was the kind of man he was looking for. He was big and strong, and had every appearance of a fighting man.

That made five he was able to get from this tribe. With his own men, that would give him thirty fighting men. If he could surprise them at the reservation, he could wipe out the soldiers, and maybe Chief Capture, while he was at it. Then he would be the chief of the tribe, the greatest warrior, and he would claim the daughter of Capture while he was there. She never would have anything to do with him, but he would take her, and she would eventually come around. She would have to!

He wished that he had a few more, but those he had picked were fierce fighting men. With surprise on his side, there would be no doubt of the outcome of the battle. Broken Nose was elated. His plans were starting to come together. All he had to do now was be sure his men were well-armed, and pick a time to attack.

When the new warriors were ready to travel, Broken Nose led the way back toward his camp. The men fell in line behind him. They were mounted on good horses that he had provided, and they kept up with him. He would take his time, and be sure they all were trained and ready to fight. It would take a little longer, but he wanted to be sure that the battle would be his when it happened.

Otter came over to his fire after he had his new men settled. "I see you have found some fighting men."

Broken Nose grinned. "Good fighting men. We will trample those pony soldiers like they were mud under our feet! Otter, I will be the chief of the tribe, and one day the chief of all the Sioux. Then I will make you chief of this tribe. You will see."

"First, you will have to get rid of some pony soldiers. You have also gotten five more fighters here since you left."

"Who are they?"

"They came from the reservation. They are pretty young, and never been in battle."

"Where are they?"

"I will get them." Otter left and soon returned with five young men.

"Broken Nose looked them over. "So you are from the reservation?"

One stepped forward. "Yes."

"Why did you come here?"

"We hate the pony soldiers, and we have heard you are the great war leader of the tribe. We want to fight with you."

"Have you ever been in battle?"

"No, but we are willing to learn."

"Can you handle a spear?"

"Yes, we are very strong."

"Are you willing to fight against your own people?"

"They will not fight us. They have no weapons, except a few Indian policemen have guns, and they will help us fight the pony soldiers."

"Good. You will train with the others. I will furnish you with some spears. Find a place to bed down."

Day after day, and as the weeks passed by, Broken Nose trained his men to charge an imagined camp, to fight hand-to-hand, and to develop a hatred for the soldiers. He was ready!

Feeling that his warriors were finally trained to fight, Broken Nose called the leader of the five reservation braves. "Where are the Indians, and where are the pony soldiers when we get there?"

"You need to come in from the east. The timber will cover you until you are very close to the fires. The first fire is where the pony soldiers stay, the next fire is the women and children, and the next is where the men sleep. Beyond that is where the wagons are, where the pony soldier chief and some of the others stay."

"You say the policemen are armed?"

"Yes."

`"Will they fight for us?"

"Yes, I'm sure they will."

"Then we shall run over the pony soldiers like a herd of buffalo over a prairie dog."

CHAPTER TEN

Looking up at the bench early one morning, Tom reviewed the progress of the last month. The warehouse was finished, the tribal building was finished, and the Agency building was well underway. When it was all done there would be a place for everyone to get in out of the weather. The soldiers would be billeted in the Agency building, the women in the tribal building, and the men in the warehouse and the barn. There were three large heating stoves, so there would be heat in all but the barn.

Up on the bench to the left of the warehouse stood thirty-one teepees, and across the valley were five more. Anderson had just reported that he had five farmers located out in the wide valley to the east. They each had a small log cabin and twenty rail-fenced acres. Anderson had allotted each farm a cow and a bull, a plow, and a harrow, and enough seed to start a garden. They would have to come in for supplies for this first year, at least. The heating stoves that he had requested for them had not arrived, and Anderson had had to build fireplaces in the cabins.

Tom and Gray Dove had grown closer by the week as they took their nightly walks down by the creek. He was in love with her, and he hoped that she felt the same. He just hadn't felt that he could talk to her about it until his future was a little more certain.

Things were looking a lot better than they had since they first came. He still had a nagging feeling that Fister had turned in a bad report to the Colonel. That could put a real twist to the donkey's tail!

Ole came up behind him. "Surveying your kingdom, are you? Ay t'ink your loyal subjects are starting to spread out. Ay vas out on the east side hunting yesterday, and a bunch of the young boys vere hunting rabbits. They had some homemade bows and arrows, and they had vun rabbit."

"Yeah, the women have been making trips to the camas meadows for roots for their pemmican. I think they're all starting to feel at home a little now. I'm trying not to feel too satisfied. The other boot could fall at any time. Ole, what are you going to do when this assignment is done?"

"Ay t'ink Ay vill be on the funny farm, bunked right next to you. Vy do you t'ink ve vill ever get away from here? Ay vill be hunting deer on my crutches, and Ay vill bring the meat in to you in your sick bed."

"Maybe if we get this place settled down, and the Indians making their own living again, we can take a plush fort job. The only trouble is I'm not sure I don't like it better here."

"Oh, Ay can see you like it better here. Ay see you every night valking that good-looking gal down to the creek. Of course, that is, if her daddy doesn't shoot you first."

Suddenly, a shot rang out down toward the fires where the soldiers were sleeping. Both men rushed to the wagon, retrieved their rifles, and started in that direction.

Tom saw the painted horde coming at him from the hill above the fires. Soldiers were all rushing to crawl under the wagons for protection, and raising their rifles to fire back. He saw two of the soldiers fall over. There were several of the Indians lying on the ground, as well.

Ole jumped under the nearest wagon and raised his rifle. Tom followed him. Were the Indians turning on them? Where did they get the horses and guns? He saw some with guns, some with bows and arrows, and some with spears. He started firing as the Indians rode past.

It was still too early to see clearly, but he fired at the shapes as they went by. He knew he hit at least one of them.

The entire Indian force rode all the way by, down the ridge past the warehouse and tribal building, and then turned and started back. Tom could see the leader as he led the group back toward him. He had a headdress of feathers falling from his head down past his shoulders. That was definitely the leader - he would try to get him as they rode past.

He held his fire until they got closer. He was aware of Ole's rifle pounding away there next to him. He would wait until the leader got near enough for a sure shot. If he got him, maybe the rest would quit. He raised his rifle, looking through the sights, then glanced back to see the Indian's progress. As the man was nearing where Tom thought would be a sure shot, he moved the sights to the left until he had the Indian in his view.

Then he got a good look. It was Broken Nose! Just as he was squeezing the trigger, Ole rose up a little and flopped over onto him. Tom looked over and saw Ole inspecting his chest, and he could see an arrow sticking out. Ole had been hit!

Tom laid down his rifle and turned the big man over on his back. "I think it missed the lung. Hang tough, partner, they'll be back."

Tom looked up toward the fires. The Indians were turning again for another run. This time the soldiers were ready, and a barrage came from under the wagons.

Once more the horde came galloping by. Tom tried to find Broken Nose in the bunch, but couldn't pick him out. He moved his sights to another Indian and knocked him off his horse. There were not nearly as many this time, and when Tom looked back up toward the fire, he could see a great many forms lying on the bench.

When the group passed the warehouse, there came a withering volley from in front of that building. The tribal police! They were shooting at the invaders, as well! That was fantastic! They could have joined the invading Indians and fought the soldiers. This had to be due to Bascomb's gaining the confidence of the police.

This last encounter threw the invaders into chaos. They wheeled around in every direction, then scattered to the winds.

Tom set his rifle down to tend to Ole. He didn't know how long the arrow was; it could be nearly all the way through. It looked as if it had penetrated quite a ways. He gently took hold of the arrow shaft. It felt pretty solid. It would be a mess trying to dig it out.

Tom rolled Ole up on his side and felt just to the inside of his shoulder blade. He thought he could feel the arrow head. "Hold on, partner. I think we'll have to take that out the back door.

He took his belt knife over to the fire and laid it across a rock against the heat. As the flames flickered over the blade, he turned it over so that they caught the other side of the blade.

Ole was again flat on his back. Tom said, "I wish that I had some whiskey for you. This is going to hurt like hell. That arrowhead is right up against your back. I'm going to have to cut it out from the back and pull it through. First, I'll have to break the shaft in two."

A shadow crossed in front of him as Bascomb walked up. "We've got two dead and two more wounded, Sir."

"How bad are the wounded?"

"One has an arrow in his side, and the other a bullet in his leg."

"Sergeant, run up to the Chief's teepee and get his wife to come down. She knows how to apply herbs that keep out the infection, then go down and brace one of your noncoms. One of them has a flask he keeps under his tunic. Tell him I don't know who he is, and we need that whiskey bad. I am sure he can find a bottle in the warehouse as well. There will be no repercussions. Then come help me with this one, and then we'll go see to the other two."

After Bascomb left, Tom cut Ole's shirt away from the shaft of the arrow. He put his hand against Ole's chest to brace it, and then the other hand just above that, grasping the arrow shaft with both hands. A stick was lying on the ground within reach. He let go the arrow and picked up the stick and stuck it in Ole's mouth.

"All right, partner, put this stick between your teeth and grit them."

He grasped the arrow shaft one more time, took a deep breath, and snapped the shaft. Ole's body arched off of the ground, he groaned, and passed out.

Turning him over gently, Tom said under his breath. "That's what we need. If I can cut out that arrow before he comes to, it will go a lot easier."

He walked over to the fire, retrieved his knife, and started a slice over the small bump made by the arrowhead. He wished that he had someone to wipe away the blood as he cut.

The point of the arrowhead was sticking out between two ribs, and Tom had to cut wider to put a wedge between the ribs to allow the head to come on through. He found a couple of sticks and sharpened them on one end, then took the handle of his knife and pounded them between the ribs until they were wide enough that he could get a finger in on each side of the arrowhead. He hooked his fingers around the back points of the arrowhead, and pulled. One of his fingers slipped off, and he had to try to insert them again in behind the arrowhead.

This time, the arrow started to move. The arrowhead scraped across the ribs, making a noise that about turned his stomach. Finally, the arrow started to move and Tom was able to pull it on through.

Blood poured out of the wound. Tom took a clean undershirt of his, cut it into strips and then bound the wounds. Ole lay there, still unconscious. Tom stood and looked down at him. "Partner, that's all I can do for you now."

He looked up and saw Bascomb hurrying down off the upper bench. He ran over to where Tom was standing. "Chief Capture has been hurt! Broken Nose was there and beat him with a club. The Chief's wife is taking care of him now. Broken Nose also captured the Chief's daughter, and rode off with her."

Gray Dove? He took Gray Dove? Tom's heart fell. Oh God! Not Gray Dove! She was his life! He couldn't live without Gray Dove!

"Which way did he go?"

"The tracks were going toward the mountains."

"Where is the soldier with the arrow?"

"He's down there by the far fire."

"Have someone saddle my horse, then come help me. I'll see if I can get the arrow out."

He was desperate to get after Gray Dove, but he couldn't just go and leave the soldier to die.

Tom ran down to the fire and examined the wounded soldier. The arrow was stuck in his side, right below the man's ribs. It wasn't in too deep, Tom thought.

He put his knife in the fire once more and then cut the man's shirt away. Putting his hands gently on the man's side, he could feel the back of the arrowhead under the skin. He said, "Soldier, hang tight - this is going to hurt, but we don't have a choice. You've got to have that thing out of there."

Some of the man's buddies were standing, watching. Tom looked up from where he was kneeling. "One of you get a clean undershirt and come wipe the blood away while I'm cutting, and hurry". He hated every second he wasn't out after Gray Dove.

Tom made a slice just over the arrowhead. The soldier arrived and started wiping the blood, as Tom increased the depth of the cut until his blade connected with the arrowhead. The soldier moaned and clenched his fists in agony. Tom widened the cut until both outer edges of the head were visible. Then he grasped the shaft of the arrow and pulled. It came out with a sucking sound, bleeding profusely.

Tom pointed to the wound. "One of you hold that undershirt on the wound, another get some strips of cloth and wrap them around his body to keep the bandage in place. Bascomb is trying to find some whiskey. Pour some of that on the wound when he gets here."

Bascomb came up the hill leading Dusty. "I went after him myself. I figured you might be in a hurry. I took time to grab some jerky, and put it in your saddle bags."

"Thanks, Bascomb. Find that whiskey and treat both of these wounded with it, inside and out. If you can, cut out the bullet in the other soldier's leg. If you can't, I'll get to it when I get back. You might pour some whiskey in his wound as well, to keep it from getting infected. Get the Chief's wife to help you with the wounded. She is a healer.

"I'll be gone until I find Gray Dove, and bring her back. I don't know how long that will take. You are in command until then. Please keep a check on Sergeant Swensen, too. Good luck."

Tom vaulted into the saddle and galloped up to the upper bench, found Broken Nose's trail and followed it.

CHAPTER ELEVEN

The tracks were easy to follow. He could see them from a gallop. Broken Nose was in a hurry and not bothering to cover his tracks. The tracks continued directly toward the mountains. Tom kept on at the fastest pace Dusty could manage. Plowing through the woods with branches swiping his face, Tom galloped over talus slopes, and waded through marshy flats where the horse's tracks could easily be seen from the saddle. Broken Nose's horse was carrying double. This should be in Tom's favor.

He climbed an open, grassy ridge, that had a narrow, hog-back spine. Here Broken Nose had stopped to rest. Tom could see moccasin tracks in the soft dirt, where the Indian had walked around, then stood watching his back trail. Gray Dove was in the clutches of that ruthless Indian! How could that be happening? It was all he could do to keep from kicking Dusty into a gallop! He didn't dare, and have Dusty give out on him.

Broken Nose knew then that he was being followed. Tom knew he would have to be more careful, for fear of an ambush. It was going to take longer than he had hoped.

Dusty was breathing heavily. Tom dismounted and loosened the cinch, and let the horse have a breather.

The country ahead was broken up with deep canyons and tall ridges running between them. The sides of the canyons were covered with tall trees, with the ridge tops mostly treeless and covered with tall grass. He could see brown rocky areas, and rock monoliths sticking skyward out of the grass.

The trail was still leading south, as it had for the last couple of hours. That probably meant that Broken Nose was heading for some hidden camp of his, and this was the direction in which it lay.

Now, Tom had to decide if it was wiser to keep following the trail, or if he might follow the ridge he was on. It was going in a southwesterly direction from where he was, but it bent around until it crossed his southerly direction off in the distance. It would be further that way, but it would all be open traveling, and maybe he could get to the point where it crossed Broken Nose's trail before they got there.

If it didn't, he would have to come all the way back here to pick up the tracks again. He picked out a small monolith on the ridge ahead where he thought the Indian's trail should cross the ridge, and got it firmly in his mind. He tightened the cinch, climbed back in the saddle, and started out along the ridge. He fervently hoped that that was the right decision. It could cost him several hours if he was wrong.

Following the ridge top was as he anticipated. There was a game trail along the very top all the way. It was open without any brush or trees to contend with, and he was able to keep Dusty at a fast walk, even though they were climbing as they progressed. It tore at his heart to think of Gray Dove in that monster's clutches.

The monolith was readily seen, as the ridge bent around to the south and then back to the east. It would not take him much longer to reach it.

When he was close, he started looking for tracks again. He rode back and forth along the ridge top, trying to see where Broken Nose had crossed it, but two passes brought no results. He tied Dusty to a small bush and started walking up and down the ridge on foot. Still, he found no tracks. He was about to think he had made the wrong decision. Broken Nose had turned aside somewhere in between.

He walked as far east as he thought he had to go to cross the trail, with no sign of tracks. He started back for Dusty. He guessed he would have to ride back to where he left the tracks. He hated that. It would give Broken Nose that much more time to get away.

There was a smooth, flat, rocky area that ran down the top of the ridge. As he started across that, he noticed a scratch on the smooth surface. Looking closer, he thought it might have been made by a horse's hoof. He walked over to the south side of the slab rock and onto the grass area beyond it. There were fresh horse tracks! He breathed a sigh of relief. He had made the right decision!

By taking the open ridge, even though it was longer, he should have gained on Broken Nose. He quickly ran to Dusty, climbed on him, and once more was on the Indian's trail.

The tracks continued in a southerly direction, and Tom pushed Dusty as fast as he could down the side of the ridge. If Broken Nose was laying for him, at least he would have to shoot uphill.

When they reached the bottom of the hill, the trail led to a narrow meadow running alongside a small creek. He didn't dare ride up the open meadow area. It would be a perfect place for Broken Nose to lie in wait and catch him out in the open. It was going to slow him down to have to ride in cover all the way along the creek, while Broken Nose could ride as fast as he wanted. There was nothing to do but do it.

Keeping in the pine timber as much as possible, Tom rode along the inner edge of the trees. There were times when he had to go out into the open to get around a thick bunch of trees. He expected to feel a bullet at any time when he had to do that.

The canyon was growing narrower, as was the strip of meadow along the creek. The canyon walls were so high that the trees on top looked small. Tom was forced out into the meadow area by a rock wall pushing out toward the creek. He stopped behind it for a moment to get his bearings. Up ahead he could see two high rock walls extending out toward him on each side of the canyon. Looking further up, he could see a similar wall stretched between the two side-walls, except they closed completely. A box canyon! That was Broken Nose's hidden camp.

He carefully looked at each wall, foot by foot. There was no break in either wall that he could see. That meant he had to go in through the mouth of the canyon. And Broken Nose could easily guard that entrance, with only one side to watch. He would have to be careful.

Easing around the rock abutment, Tom held Dusty to a slow walk, while he searched every opening ahead of him for signs of the Indian and Gray Dove. Every time he was forced out into the open, he stopped first and surveyed the country ahead of him. He knew he was close to Broken Nose's camp.

He couldn't stand the thought of Gray Dove in the clutches of that renegade, but he had to steel himself to go cautiously. It wouldn't help her any if he got himself killed.

The two side-walls towered over him as he came to the mouth of the box canyon. The walls had crowded in toward the creek until there was little bottom land on either side. He could almost throw a rock and hit either wall.

He dismounted and tied Dusty to a tree. He pulled his rifle from the scabbard and then thought better of it. It was too narrow in here for a rifle. It would be an encumbrance more than a help. He put it back.

The hoof prints were closer together now. Broken Nose wasn't feeling the pressure of pursuit. Maybe the Indian thought he had lost him.

The canyon bottom was getting brushy as Tom entered the box canyon mouth. The trail along the creek was open, but that was a sure way to walk into an ambush. Tom wound his way through the brush at the edge of the canyon wall, taking careful steps not to walk on any dry branch or loose rock that could give him away. The camp had to be close. The end wall of the box was not that far away.

Every step now was bringing him closer to the Indian and Gray Dove. He was drawing now on every skill he had learned over the years as an army scout.

Tom drew his pistol. It was so quiet. There were no bird songs, or animal rustling, only the burble of the creek as it flowed by.

A rock inclusion stood out from the wall, and sloped out from the canyon wall almost to the creek. It had collapsed over time and sloped in steps from the top of the canyon wall to the canyon bottom, a few feet from the creek. Tom stepped carefully around it, searching the canyon bottom ahead of him inch by inch. He turned to his left, and saw an overhang deep enough to cast a dark shadow on the interior. Remains of campfires were on the ground in front of the overhang.

Tom strained to see inside and thought he could make out Gray Dove lying there. He started toward the opening, and a premonition hit him. He looked up just in time to see Broken Nose jumping from the ledge onto him. Tom tried to swing his pistol up, but the Indian hit him before he could. The blow knocked him over, and as he hit the ground, his hand struck a rock, knocking the pistol from his hand.

His hand felt numb, and he rolled onto his back to meet the thrust of Broken Nose's knife. Tom raised his good hand up and grabbed the descending arm. The long knife in the Indian's hand was poised right above his chest, and Tom struggled to keep it from plunging into him.

Broken Nose grabbed Tom by the throat with his other hand, and choked him until he couldn't get his breath. Tom felt with his numb hand for his belt knife. He had to turn up on his side to reach it. The Indian was heavy, and a red film began to cover Tom's eyes before he could get his knife out. His lungs were screaming for air.

Tom was able to get his feet planted, and he heaved up, tossing Broken Nose to the ground. Both men jumped to their feet. Tom's head was swimming, and he was having trouble focusing his eyes. Broken Nose saw Tom's knife and stepped back to watch for a rush from the soldier. It gave Tom time enough to bring his eyesight back into focus.

Broken Nose made a rush at Tom, his knife extended. Tom barely had time to twist out of the way. He slashed down with his knife, hitting the Indian's uprising arm. Broken Nose jumped back. The two circled around, thrusting and blocking, both men bleeding from cuts to the arms and sides.

Broken Nose made a charge with his knife extended. Tom was able to grab the arm as it came at him and thrust it to the side, but the charge carried both of them into the creek. Broken Nose wound up straddling Tom, and held his face under the water.

Struggling for breath, Tom squirmed and heaved, trying to get the man off of him. He had hold of the Indian's knife arm and didn't dare let go of that His own knife arm was pinned under the other's leg.

Tom held his breath as long as he could, but the urge to let his breath go was getting excruciating. The pressure built up until Tom knew he was going to have to gasp for breath, and that would mean taking in a lung full of water. He had to do something, and quick!

With a last effort, Tom swung a leg up and got it around the front of the Indian's neck and slammed him over backward into the water.

Struggling to catch his breath, Tom jumped to his feet, as did Broken Nose, and the two started circling again. Tom thrust his knife at Broken Nose, and the blade entered the man's buckskin shirt. Tom tried to turn the blade to inflict some damage, but Broken Nose fell away. Tom jumped forward, attempting to pin the man down, but the Indian was too nimble and jumped to the side.

Once more Broken Nose thrust his knife at Tom. Tom twisted, but felt the knife hit his ribs. He brought his own knife hard up into the man's belly just below the ribs, and felt the Indian sink to the ground.

Tom stepped back waiting for Broken Nose to rise, but he rolled over on his back, his eyes sightless. Tom sank to the ground, totally exhausted.

When he could get his breath again, he rose and walked over to the overhang. He could see Gray Dove lying there, bound up and with a gag over her mouth. He hurried over and removed that, then untied her.

Gray Dove thrust her arms around his neck. "Oh. Tom, I was so scared! I thought he would kill you!"

"Are you all right?"

"Yes, I'm not hurt. I'm so glad to see you! How did you know where to find me?"

"Let's talk about that later. Do you think you can ride?"

"Yes, I can ride."

"We'd better move out. Some of his men got away from the battle in the compound. They could be coming in here at any time."

Tom helped her to her feet and held her tight for a minute, then went back out, picked up his pistol, and retrieved Broken Nose's horse. He helped Gray Dove onto the horse, then, led it out of the box canyon and down the canyon bottom to where he had tied Dusty.

They rode side by side down the meadow along the creek. It was so quiet, it seemed surreal.

A horse and rider appeared down the creek a good ways off. Tom grabbed her horse's bridle, and reined Dusty off to the side of the trail. He got the two horses out of sight in the trees, and dismounted. Grabbing the rifle from its scabbard, Tom inched his way to a tree at the edge of the meadow, and waited.

The rider ambled up the meadow, and when he approached where Tom was hiding, Tom stepped out, the rifle pointed directly at the Indian's belly. "Raise your hands!"

Tom could see that he didn't understand English, and he motioned with his rifle barrel. That message got through.

After the first shock of seeing Tom, standing with a rifle trained on him, the Indian looked for some means of escape. He kept looking from side to side, muscles tensed, and ready to kick his horse in the ribs if he could see the slightest waiver in the barrel of that gun.

Keeping the rifle trained on the man, Tom hollered to Gray Dove to bring the horses out. She led Dusty and her horse out of the trees, and when they got to where Tom was standing, he asked her to get a piggin'-string from his saddle bag.

With the string in hand, Gray Dove held on to the reins of both horses and handed Tom the string. He quickly handed her his rifle, and tied the Indian's hands in front of him. Then Tom searched the man for weapons and found a Henry rifle, and a knife.

Waiting until the man was securely tied, Gray Dove, recognizing him as one of the young men who had left the burial grounds, approached him. "Why did you leave the Chief and join a renegade like Broken Nose?"

"Broken Nose is a great warrior. Someday, I will be a great warrior, too. Chief Capture and the other Indians will see how great a chief I am."

"You are foolish! Broken Nose was a false chief. He was no good. He would do nothing but get you killed. He is dead now, and can do no more harm."

The threat of more of Broken Nose's warriors made Tom decide to leave the valley floor and tackle the long hillside. He pointed out to the captive where he wanted him to go, and then he and Gray Dove followed.

It was steep going and they had to rest the horses often before they reached the top. Tom attempted to follow game trails as they progressed up the incline, to try to take advantage of a lesser grade. The horses struggled with the steep slope and rocky footing.

Once there, the open ridge top that Tom had ridden before lay ahead of them. It was easy going along the top of the ridge, and they made good time.

Darkness caught them before they reached the crossing where they had to leave the ridge top. Tom pushed on as long as they could, but finally had to call a halt.

A lone juniper stood near the trail they were following. Tom stopped there, helped the Indian off his horse, then walked him over to the tree and tied his hands behind him and around the tree. He left enough slack so that the man could sit on the ground. He tied the two horses to another tree a little further down the trail.

His jerky supply was a little short, but he brought all of it back to where Gray Dove was waiting. He split it three ways, handed her a portion, laid his own on a rock, and brought the last over to the Indian. He held it in front of the Indian's mouth and gestured for him to take it. The Indian shook his head, and Tom tried again. Again, he got a negative signal. Tom sat on the ground and waited. Then, he tried once more and the Indian opened his mouth and Tom inserted a piece of jerky. He waited until the Indian had eaten the first piece and inserted another, until the entire portion was gone. Then he walked back over to where Gray Dove was sitting and ate his own.

When they had eaten, Gray Dove said, "Now, Mr. Soldier, how did you find me? I thought I would never see you again, it was so far back in the mountains."

"I was right behind you all the way. I just followed his tracks, and when I saw where he was heading, I took a short cut and caught up with you right after he made his camp."

Tom pointed to the Indian. "Was this one a member of the group that left the reservation?"

"Yes, he and four others."

"I thought I recognized two of them that didn't make it through the attack. There may have been others that escaped."

Tom led her over to a large boulder, sat down leaning against it, and pulled her down to him. They sat with his arms around her, giving what comfort he could.

"Are you all right? You are mighty quiet."

"My father. Is he all right? Broken Nose was beating him with a club before he took me away."

"I don't know for sure. Your mother was tending to him when I left, and he was still alive then."

Sergeant Bascomb walked up to Tom's wagon when he saw them ride in. "Did you get Broken Nose?"

"He's dead. I need something to do with this one, though. Any suggestions?"

"We have five prisoners. Two of them are wounded and they're up in the tribal building. I had Anderson and Riley take their crews and build a jail. The rest of them are in there."

"Good work, Sergeant. Would you put this one in there, also? I'm taking Gray Dove up to her parents, and I want to meet with you and your noncoms after that to assess our situation. How is Ole?"

"That tough Swede - you couldn't kill him with a cannon. He'll live."

There was a pot of hot coffee on the fire when he got back from the Chief's teepee. The old chief was going to make it, but he had been battered pretty badly by the renegade. Gray Dove had stayed to help her mother.

The coffee felt pretty good going down, and he sat by the fire enjoying it until Bascomb and his crew arrived.

Bascomb sat next to him. "Lieutenant, we lost two of our boys in the scrape. There's five more wounded. We have them up in the hospital."

"Hospital! What hospital?"

"You had the cots set up for the older women in the tribal building. We moved enough of them for the wounded to one end, and put up a dividing wall between them and the rest of the room. The Indian women are tending to them. It's our makeshift hospital."

"Has there been any other hostility from the Indians we brought in here?"

"No, in fact they have all been very helpful. Even attending our wounded, as well as their own."

"Very good, Sergeant. You have done an excellent job in assuming command here. I'll mention it in my next report. Please give my thanks to all of your men, including the tribal police. They could have turned on us, instead of the Broken Nose bunch. Tell them I am grateful. My thanks to all of you. Now go take a much-deserved rest, if you can."

The next stop was his new hospital. He was amazed when he walked into the building. One corner had been cordoned off and the cots were lined up in the walled-off room, with space for the helpers to get between.

Tom walked down the line, checking with every one, soldiers and reservation Indians alike. He shook their hands and said a few words, whether they could understand him or not. He thought they realized that at the least he was wishing them good luck.

The last bed he went to was Ole's. "I've heard of some lazy soldiers in my time, but this is the limit. Lay here in this bed, with one hundred and fifty good- looking women to wait on you. Aren't you ashamed of yourself?"

Ole grinned. "Ay t'ink Ay've found yust the yob for old retired scouts. They look after you like a baby - the only t'ing is the veeds they put on you smells like skunk cabbage!"

"That isn't the weeds; that's the orneriness coming out through that wound. How are you doing?"

"Yust about as good as Ay could be. It is sore, but Ay don't t'ink it is infected. Ay need to get up."

"No, you don't. Not until nurses say you are healed. Now get some rest. I'm going down to the wagon and do the same."

Tom walked back to his wagon, lay down underneath it and collapsed, completely exhausted.

The next morning after all the crews were back at their assigned tasks, Tom looked up Bascomb.

"Sergeant, I have a question for you. The tribal police, on their own, stood off the raiders down on that end of the compound. Are they capable now of operating on their own, without the direction from the soldiers?"

"Yes, Sir. They are practically doing that now."

"Then, I think I will turn them over to the chief, and make it purely a tribal operation. That would leave your soldiers to just patrol the boundaries. How does that strike you?"

"I think it's a good idea. They are very proud of their force. They can monitor the Indians on the reservation land. We have a jail now, they can incarcerate the miscreants. We can always revert back to supervising them if it becomes necessary."

"Good. I'll see the chief today and tell him. You tell the police chief. I think that will please them. Thanks, Sergeant."

Tom made his way then up to the teepee of the chief - and of his daughter.

A fire was burning brightly in the teepee when Tom entered. Horse Capture was sitting wrapped in a blanket on the other side of the fire, and Maple Leaf and Gray Dove were sitting on each side of him. He waved to Tom to take a seat across from them.

Gray Dove smiled at Tom. "My father says thank you for bringing me back. I want to thank you once more for doing that. He also wants to thank you for ridding the tribe of Broken Nose. He would always have caused problems for everyone. I don't know what would have happened to me if you hadn't done all of that. It wouldn't have been anything good."

"Tell your father that I was as anxious to have you back as he was. That is something I want to talk to you about tonight, if you are up for a walk."

Gray Dove and her father talked for a bit, while Tom shifted a little uncomfortably across the fire.

Finally Tom said, "Gray Dove I want to talk to your father about the tribal police. Sergeant Bascomb has trained them to the point he feels that they are seasoned enough to act on their own.

"As you know, my main responsibility to the Army is to keep the Indians on the reservation. My responsibility to myself is to keep them as well and as happy as I know how. I am proposing that your father take over the managing of the tribal police. Make it a tribal function. He and his council can oversee it. I will still have the final responsibility for their actions, but if something comes up, I will go through him to correct it. They proved themselves when they stood up to Broken Nose's warriors along with the soldiers."

Once again Gray Dove and her father had a long conversation. After he had finished talking, she turned back to Tom. "My father said he appreciates the honor you are giving him, and he will take the responsibility for the tribal police. The people will appreciate having their own police dealing with the lawbreakers."

"That's good. Then I can put my soldiers back to patrolling the reservation." He stood. "Thank your father for me, and I will see you tonight."

When Tom arrived back at his wagon, Ole was sitting by the fire waiting for him. Tom picked up a cup and poured a cup of coffee. "Aren't you a little frisky so soon? How's the shoulder?"

"Better. Ay can move my arm pretty vell now. Pretty Rose says Ay have to keep my arm in a sling for a veek or so. But it yust gets in the vay all the time."

A clatter of hooves got their attention. Five soldiers rode up to the wagon at a gallop. They dismounted and a soldier in a lieutenant's uniform, walked over to where Tom and Ole were sitting. "Are you Lieutenant Colter?"

Tom stood and walked over to shake his hand. "Yes, I'm Tom Colter."

"Lieutenant Colter, I am Lieutenant John Davis. I have been instructed to take you back to the fort to stand trial."

"Stand trial? For what?"

"I can't say for sure. I've heard them say incompetence, poor judgment, disobeying an order, among other things. I don't know what the charges will be. General Hadley is there and ordered the trial. They want us to return immediately."

"Can't it wait until morning? In my incompetence, I would like to tie up a few loose ends before I go. You can turn your horses into the corral, down there by the barn. The soldiers are bedded down right over there by the wagons and the big fire. Feel free to join them. Lieutenant, you may have supper with Ole and me tonight, if you wish."

That evening, Tom had three meals brought up to his wagon from the cook fire. When Lieutenant Davis joined them for supper, Tom handed him a plate of pemmican, some watercress, and beans.

"Here you go, Lieutenant. Standard fare for reservation soldiers."

"What is this brown material, and the greens?"

"The brown is pemmican. The Indian women mix what grain we were furnished with camas roots, deer and buffalo meat that has been smoked, and store it for the winter. The greens are watercress that they have retrieved from the creek down there. It all gets to be right tasty after a while."

Davis looked very skeptical at first, but finally managed to get it down, and gladly accepted the coffee Tom poured for him.

Davis said, "I took the liberty of inspecting your facility when I took the horses to the corral. I see that you have built a barn, a warehouse, and another building where the Indian women are staying. You have also started another building. What is it for?"

"That will be the soldiers' quarters when it's finished. We hope to have it done before cold weather sets in."

"There were about thirty teepees on the bench by the buildings, and I thought I saw some across the valley. Who is in those?"

"You have good eyes. Those are the homes of the Indians that the tribal council has allotted to the families that they felt needed them the most. The tepees are made from the animals that Master Sergeant Swensen, here, and his men have been able to kill. The tepee by itself is occupied by the chief. I have asked him to take it and use it as a tribal council building until we can get one built. He needs somewhere he can meet with the people individually."

"I counted around fifty head of cattle in the corral. Is that correct?"

"Yes."

"Is that the extent of your facilities?"

"We have five farms in the eastern part of the reservation. They each have a log cabin, twenty acres that have been fenced, and two head of cattle, a bull and a cow."

"All right, Lieutenant Colter. I will include all of that in my report."

"Then, I will leave you for the evening and be ready to go with you in the morning." Tom stood and left for the single tepee on the bench.

Lieutenant Davis stood looking after Tom, then turned to Swensen. "Can he be trusted? You don't think he'll run away?"

Ole laughed. "If half of the men in this army could be trusted as much as that man, ve vould have twice as good an army as ve have. He'll be here and ready to go ven you're ready."

Gray Dove came running down from the bench, when she saw Tom coming. He took her hand and walked her down to the creek, and to their favorite spot under the pine tree. They sat with their backs to the tree, watching the water cascade over the rocks.

Tom sat staring at the water, and Gray Dove waited for him to say something. Finally, she put a hand on his shoulder. "Tom, is something wrong? You haven't said a word since we got here."

"I'm sorry. I have something to say to you, and I don't know just how to start. You know I love you, don't you?"

"I have been hoping so. I love you, too."

"I intended to bring you down here tonight and ask you to marry me. Now, something has come up that won't let me."

"What is it, Tom? What could it be?"

"Lieutenant Davis from the fort came in with four soldiers today. They have sent him to bring me back to stand trial. I'll have to leave in the morning."

"Stand trial for what?"

"According to Davis, I am charged with incompetence, neglect of duties, not following orders, and I am not sure what else."

"Why have they done that? You've been the best to our people that anybody could be with the job they gave you to do."

"I tried to do the best I knew how. We'll just have to wait and see what they come up with. I don't know what will come of it all. I might be discharged from the army, maybe even thrown in jail, if they decide it is serious enough. At any rate, I can't ask you to marry me with that hanging over my head. I might be put away for a long time."

"It's not fair! But whatever their decision is, I'll be here waiting for you." She reached over and kissed him.

They sat talking until after dark. Finally, Tom said. "I hate to leave, but I need to get ready to travel in the morning. I'd better take you home."

He kissed her long and tenderly when they arrived at the tepee. "'Bye, Sweetheart, wish us luck." He turned and walked down the hill to his wagon.

She whispered, "Goodbye, Tom", under her breath as she watched him walk back to his wagon.

Ole was sitting, waiting for him when he arrived. "Did you tell the fair maiden that you vere a criminal, and you vouldn't be seeing her anymore?"

"Yes. She said that that didn't matter, that she knew a Swede up by the wagons that she could latch on to. I told her that was all right, but she had better do it fast, because I would probably do away with him before morning. One thing I need to tell that Swede is that starting in the morning he will be in charge of this outfit until I get back, or whoever takes my place gets back. I don't know of anything special that needs done, just carry on with our usual activities.

"I don't think I told Bascomb that the chief agreed to take over the tribal police and for him to inform the police to report to the chief, hereafter. Oh, scratch that, I did tell him. I think they better put me away for losing my mind. Anyhow, if something comes up that needs their attention, tell the chief to take care of it, unless it is something the soldiers need to do. Good luck."

CHAPTER TWELVE

It took most of two days to make the trip back to the fort. Tom felt like a prisoner. He was riding in front with Davis, and the soldiers rode in formation right behind him. They opened the gates for them, and Davis rode directly over to the Commandant's office, motioning Tom to follow him.

They dismounted and walked onto the porch and into the office. Colonel Brewster was sitting behind a large desk at the far end of the room. He rose, walked around the desk, and shook Tom's hand. "Tom, I'm glad to see you. I'm sorry about all of this. Have a chair.

"Davis, as soon as you have your report written up, take it to General Hadley. He'll want to review it before morning. I'll see you then. Tom, stand by for a little. I want to talk to you."

Davis left the room, and Brewster went back to his seat behind the desk. "Tom, I want you to know, this wasn't my idea. I tried to talk the general out of it, but when Fister came in with his report, the general was present. When he heard the Indians were nowhere to be seen, he hit the ceiling and called for a court martial. I will help any way I can, but I hope you have a good explanation. I would like to talk to you about it, but I am on the review panel, so I can't. I do want you to know that I have every confidence in you, and remain your friend.

"Go over to the officer's quarters and get something to eat and a good night's sleep. We will convene here in this office at ten in the morning" He rose and shook Tom's hand again. "Good luck, Tom."

"Thank you, Sir, I appreciate that."

Tom entered the officer's quarters. He felt a little funny going in there. All of the time he had served here as a scout, he had slept in the enlisted men's barracks. He cleaned up some, and by then it was chow time. He went to the mess hall, ate, and returned to try to sleep. It seemed to him that every eye in the place was on him while he was eating. That made him feel like a criminal, even though he wasn't.

Sleep didn't come until far into the night. His mind kept turning all of this over and over, trying to come up with some explanation.

At least for tonight he was in a private room and sleeping in an honest-to-gosh bed.

A table had been set up in the colonel's headquarters, with three chairs behind it. The general was sitting in the middle, with Brewster on his right, and a member of the general's staff on the left.

Tom saluted. "Lieutenant Tom Colter reporting, Sir."

The general shuffled some papers. "Take a chair in back of that table, Lieutenant. We will wait until everyone is present."

While he was waiting, Tom surveyed the room. The colonel's desk was at the back of the room, a United States flag on the wall on one side of the desk, the Ninth Cavalry flag on the other. The hearing table where the General and Brewster were seated was directly in front of the desk, with the three chairs behind it. Tom's table was directly in front of the hearing table. He had been in this room many times, but never had he felt as uncomfortable as he did now.

Several more officers came in and took chairs that had been placed in the room. Finally, the general looked over at Tom.

"Lieutenant, you have been brought here on the charges of dereliction of duties. I, myself, have made the charges. You were given the responsibility for moving approximately three hundred and fifty Indians to an area designated as a reservation for them, and to hold them there until you had further orders.

"I was here when the officer charged with bringing supplies to the reservation came back. He reported that there was not a single Indian in sight at the compound, and that your soldiers were lounging around the fires.

"He stated further that you had sent a soldier out with several of the Indians, who had been given guns, to hunt off the reservation, all the while not killing any of the cattle that had been sent to you for feeding the Indians.

"And with disregard for the safety of the soldiers, you armed another group of the Indians.

"He further stated that you had built a barn, a warehouse, and a tribal building instead of building shelters for the Indians.

"I can't think of a more despicable disregard of orders, and demonstration of a lack of judgment of an officer who had the trust of his superiors, than you have shown. Colonel Brewster recommended you highly before you were given this responsibility, and I have to question his judgment in picking you for the job.

"I don't see any way that you can justify these actions, but you have a chance now to try."

Tom stood and faced the officers.

"Thank you, Sir. I would like to start first with the buildings. The corrals were built to hold the cattle that the army brought in. With winter coming on, we had to have a place to store the hay to feed them this winter. Private Riley was given five Indians to cut the timber and build the barn to hold the hay. The steers were not butchered because we will need them this winter when we can't get out to hunt.

"If we had not gone out to hunt, we would have run out of meat a month ago, when the second bunch of cattle were supposed to have come in from the army. They still haven't arrived. To counter this problem in the future, we intend to keep the cows to form a herd over the next five years that will support the needs of the reservation, and not have to depend on the questionable deliveries from the outside. It will provide jobs for many of the tribal men, and maybe in the future, we can trade the army meat for grain.

"Private Thoreson was given five Indians, picked by the chief, to build the warehouse. This was needed to protect the supplies that were brought in. This gave us a way to portion out the food as needed, and to protect it from the weather.

"When this was finished, he and his crew built the tribal building. It was the only way we could provide shelter and heat in the coming winter. These people had nothing but the clothes on their backs when they got there. They had no weapons to hunt for meat, and no hides with which to build their teepees. We had only three stoves to heat the supplies, three hundred and fifty Indians, plus thirty soldiers. We divided the men, some sleep in the warehouse, some in the barn. The women sleep in the tribal house, and the soldiers will sleep in the agency building when it is finished. There will be heat in the warehouse, the tribal building, and the agency building.

"Thirty tepees have been constructed by the tribal women, and families have been assigned to them by the chief. We hope to have enough hides for twenty more before snowfall. When this is done, these families moving out of the big buildings will allow room for the men sleeping in the barn to move into the warehouse where there will be heat. The families in the tepees can have fires in their homes, as they traditionally have.

"Now, as to arming some of the Indians, Sergeant Bascomb was given the task of training a group of the Indians who were picked by the chief to form a tribal police unit. He assigned one of them to each of the patrolling soldiers. They taught them to shoot, to take care of their guns, and how to act as an officer. When the raid came, instead of them turning their guns on us, they were right there with the soldiers, firing on the raiders, even though the raiders were Sioux, also.

"Master Sergeant Swensen did the same with the hunters assigned to him. They have provided the meat needed to last a part of the winter, and the hides to build the thirty teepees.

"Now, the missing Indians. I have developed what I believe to be a mutual respect and understanding with Chief Capture. He is a very honorable man, and his word is always good. He has control of his tribe. His word is the law in the tribe. He asked me if they could have the burial of one of the young boys in the tribe in private, and to be held in the burial ground that he and I had picked out for the tribe.

"He assured me that they would all return to the compound. I realized that if they didn't it would probably be my career, but I have every faith in Chief Capture, and I granted him his wish.

"The soldiers "lounging around" that Mr. Fister was concerned with had just arrived back from a two-day patrol of the boundary, and were resting from that.

"I believe that I acted in the best interest of the Indian people and the army. Thank you."

The general looked over at Brewster, and then down at some notes he had taken. "Lieutenant Colter, I believe you have adequately answered everything but the most serious charge: Letting the Indians completely out of the sight of the soldiers that were there to keep them contained. In view of that, I think ...."

At that moment, the outer door opened and Chief Capture and Gray Dove stepped into the room. They walked over in front of the table that the officers were sitting behind.

Gray Dove looked up at the officers. "Gentlemen, I am Gray Dove. This is my father, Chief Horse Capture. He has asked me to read his statement to you, if you are willing."

The general said, "Well, this is unusual, but if it applies to this case, go ahead."

Gray Dove unfolded a paper, and began to read. "You, the pony soldiers, waged war on our tribe and killed many of our brothers and sisters. You marched us to this fort and held us in a pen until you were ready to ship us to the reservation.

"You gave this man the responsibility to march us to that place, and hold us there as captives. Our people hated the pony soldiers who had killed our people and held us in captivity. This included Lieutenant Colter, and all the others.

"We had no weapons to hunt with, no means of shelter against the winter months, and nothing of our own but the clothes on our backs.

"As we marched, I noticed that Lieutenant Colter kept the march slow to make it easier for the old and young to keep up easily, and let us rest often. My wife became too tired to walk, and he took her up on the seat of the wagon he was driving.

"When we came to the river, I expected the pony soldiers to make us wade the river, but the Lieutenant drove all the wagons across while we rested. He had them emptied and then made numerous trips back and forth through the water to haul us across. Once across, they fed us and let us rest there for the night. Then, the next day, they reloaded the wagons and we proceeded.

"I began to see that he truly cared for our welfare. When we arrived at the reservation, he met with me often to craft the best way to meet the needs of our people, both at the present and in the future. He has put our people to work making things better, rather than just keeping them herded in a pen.

"Because of all of this, the people are looking at the reservation as their new home, and working side by side with the pony soldiers to make life better. We no longer look at them as keepers, but as friends.

"Lieutenant Colter is a man of his word. He has shown respect and compassion for our people. He has restored us some dignity. He has my complete trust, and I would never do anything to taint the trust he has placed in me. As I promised him, we all returned to the campsite after the burial ceremony for our young boy.

"I thank you for listening to me."

The general stood. "Thank you, Chief Capture. We shall take note of your words. There will be a brief recess, and we will meet back here in one-half hour."

Chief Capture and Gray Dove turned and left the room, and the others present followed. The general and his fellow hearing officers retired to the colonel's quarters to confer.

Tom remained seated at his table, going over and over the charges and testimony, trying to get some sense of what the outcome might be.

When they had reconvened, General Hadley remained standing. "Lieutenant Colter, please stand. When I called this hearing, I expected at the very least to terminate your service, with a bad conduct rating. I thought you to be the very worst example of what an officer in this army should be.

"I cannot say that I condone all of your methods, but now that I have a better understanding of the relationship that you were able to develop with the chief and his people, I believe that you probably have done the best job of setting up a reservation that we have seen since this conflict started. You have made the people feel like it is their home, not being held prisoner, as has been the case all too often, and have shown respect for their needs.

"Therefore, Instead of disciplinary action I am recommending you for a commendation. And please accept my apology."

Tom said, "Thank you sir, but much of what we were able to accomplish was due to the efforts of Sergeants Swensen and Bascomb, and Privates Thoreson, Riley, and Anderson. Any commendation should include them.

"There should also be mention of the cooperation and understanding of Chief Capture, and the interpretation given us by his daughter, Gray Dove. Thank you once more."

When the meeting broke up, Colonel Brewster came over to where Tom was standing.

"Congratulations, Tom. This will go on your record, and I would guess another promotion may not be too long coming."

"I would like to see one coming for the men I named, Sir. They have done a terrific job."

When they left the building, Gray Dove and the chief were waiting. Tom shook the chief's hand. "I can't tell you how much I appreciate your coming. I think I would not have made it without your testimony."

"Father says that he is glad. He wants you back on the reservation."

"Tell him that first I am going to steal something from him. I would like him to give his daughter to me, when the colonel marries us."

She talked to the chief, and he smiled, then reached up and hugged his future son-in-law.

CHAPTER THIRTEEN

Pulling Gray Dove through the door behind him, Tom walked over to the end of the porch. "What are your plans? Is your father going to stay here until after we are married? Where will you stay? Sorry about all the questions, but I haven't had time to think about these things with the trial and all."

"My plans are to marry some criminal soldier. Yes, my father will stay long enough for us to get married. Mrs. Brewster asked me to stay with them. Let's see, were there any other questions?"

"Yes, why are you waiting so long to kiss me?"

He put his arms around her and held her tight for a long time. "I don't know how you can be so far down in a hole one minute and higher than the stars the next. Right now, I can't get my mind wrapped around what I should do next."

"You said something about a kiss."

There was no conversation for several minutes after that.

Tom finally released her. "I guess the first thing I need to do is find Brewster and see where I go from here. Whether I'm to go back to the reservation, when that will be, and see if he will marry us before we go."

He kissed her again and left for Brewster's office. Gray Dove rejoined her father.

The orderly asked Tom to wait when he asked to see the colonel. Tom took a chair at one side of the room, and discussed the latest happenings around the fort with the orderly while he waited. The door to Brewster's office opened and Brewster and the general came out. The general walked over to Tom.

"Lieutenant, I'm leaving to go back east now, but I want to express my apologies for doubting you, and for hauling you in for the trial, but it is the first time I have heard of a soldier having that much trust in a captive, and making it work! I will have some stories to tell them back there. Congratulations, and keep up the good work."

The general turned to leave, and Brewster started to follow. "Tom, wait here. I'll be back shortly."

When Brewster returned he motioned Tom to follow him into his office. He waved him into a chair by his desk. "Tom, you have my apologies as well. I'm sorry you had to go through that. I want you to know I never wanted it to happen."

"I know, Sir. I know there would have been some conversation between us before you called for a trial. I came in to find out what you wanted me to do next. Do I go back to the reservation, and when? Also, I am in love with the girl who translated for the chief, and I wanted to ask you if you would marry us?"

"I won't marry you. We have a perfectly good preacher right here at the fort, and besides that, I am planning to be your best man."

"My best man! You knew I was going to ask you to marry us?"

"Tom, you are going to be a married man soon. You will soon learn that when a couple of women get together, just get out of the way! Rosalyn and Gray Dove have been together for two days and a night now. I doubt if Gray Dove had been in the house for ten minutes before Rosalyn had wormed out of her that you two were wanting to get married. I don't doubt that the wedding is mostly planned and all the king's horses are rounded up to participate.

"Now, as to the reservation, I do want you to return. I am really pleased with what you have done there, and I would like to see it completed before you go somewhere else. It would be nice to have one reservation that was working like it should be, and I would like very much to have it be one under my command.

"As to timing, I want you to move your gear over to the married officer's quarters. There is an empty bungalow there, and you and Gray Dove will have the use of that for a week before you head back after the ceremony. It's not much of a honeymoon here on the fort, but I have a hunch you will make the most of it."

He reached down into a drawer in his desk, and pulled out a small bottle of whiskey. "I keep this for special occasions, and this is surely one of them."

He produced two glasses from the same drawer and filled them. One of them went to Tom and the Colonel raised his glass. "To you, Tom, and to your bride."

Shaking hands with the colonel, and trying to get his mind around all that was happening to him, Tom made his way to the barracks, gathered up his gear, and went out in search of the bungalow.

'Bungalow', Tom decided, might be stretching things just a little. It was a barracks building that had been made into six apartments, but better than anything he had lived in since he left home. There was a kitchen, small living room, and a bedroom. The kitchen had a stove, sink, a cupboard, and a table with four chairs. The living room had a fireplace, and four easy chairs. The floor was partially covered with a well-worn rug. The bedroom had a large double bed, a dresser, and a closet. The officers lived in style!

Tom put his clothes in the dresser, then, made his way to the colonel's quarters and knocked. Rosalyn Brewster opened the door. Tom doffed his hat. "Mrs. Brewster, is Gray Dove here?"

"I'm going to tell you right now, Mister. This place is off limits to you, and any other man for that matter, until the wedding. We have so many things to take care of we don't need any meddling by outsiders. Go back over to the barracks and tell tall tales about your battles, or something. Now git!" She did say it with a smile, but there was an undercurrent of steel behind it. Tom left.

Wandering around the compound, he looked for something to do. Most of the soldiers were out on patrol, or carrying on their duties here at the fort. The barracks were empty. Tom finally went down to the stables and found a sympathetic horse and started currying him down.

"Old horse, we're a pair. Nothing to do when we could be out roaming around the country seeing new things, and all we can do is look at the inside of this fort and wait for time to pass."

He put down the curry comb, went into the tack room, took down a saddle and bridle and a blanket and went back to the horse. "It's time we did something about this."

Getting the horse saddled took only a few minutes and he was soon mounted and at the gates asking the guard to open them. Once through, he turned north and let the horse pick his own speed as they proceeded out onto the prairie.

As many sojourns as he had made as a scout, he had never been in this direction. Soon the prairie land turned to a series of canyon lands and ridges. Large cliffs extended for miles and forced him to take the way dictated by the direction in which they lay. There was no way to gain access to the top of them.

A rocky monolith arose off in the distance. Tom rode toward it. When he reached the base of the uplift, he stopped, dismounted and loosened the cinch on the saddle. He ground-reined the horse and then climbed up the steep, rocky rise before him. When he arrived at the summit, he sat down on a large boulder and viewed the expanse of prairie land all around him.

It felt good to get out away from mankind for a little while. It was good for the soul. He and Ole had lived in this environment for years, and it was good to get back to it. He was out in the open when he was at the reservation, but it wasn't the same. Still he had Gray Dove at the reservation. He guessed there were trade-offs that needed to be considered.

When he had rested long enough, he made his way back down to the horse and cinched up again. He'd ride on in the same direction for another half hour and then he had better start back. Soon, he approached a long, red-colored cliff that extended easterly across his path. He decided to follow it for a ways.

The cliff he was following gradually turned further eastward, forcing Tom to turn that direction as well. The heat from the sun bounced off of the cliff, and soon man and horse were sweating from the temperature. Tom found a small area where the cliff turned enough to provide some shade from the sun. He reined the horse over to it and then stopped in the shelter of the cliff to try to cool off some.

Sitting there in the shade of the cliff, the reservation and all of its problems seemed far away. What were Gray Dove and Rosalyn Brewster doing that was all that secret? He just felt like a big fifth wheel on a rickety farm wagon. He picked up a rock and threw it at a prickly pear cactus and one lobe fell off onto the ground. "That's the way I feel, cactus. Just like I was hit and knocked off the world."

What was happening on the reservation? Was Ole making things work all right? Had they finished the Agency building? How could they be managing without him there to look after things?

He thought he got a whiff of smoke. He looked around and couldn't see any. Tom got to his feet and walked around the point in the cliffs ahead of him. The odor was a little stronger there. As he kept on in that direction, he would get the smell every now and then.

The cliffs made another small turn to his left and he could see a dark slit in the cliff face ahead of him. When he reached the slit, it turned out to be a cleft running straight back from the cliff face. It was about fifty feet wide, and the vertical walls on each side rose several hundred feet high, to the height of the cliff he had been following.

A rocky, dry creek bed was in the center of the canyon, and the floor of the canyon was choked with salt cedar, sagebrush, rabbit brush and grass. It was obvious that at times a small stream ran through here, and that there was water underground even now that was feeding the vegetation. It probably was near the surface where the roots could reach it.

Tom eased over to the mouth of the canyon. The odor of smoke was stronger here, and he thought he could detect a thin smoke color in the air. It must be coming from the canyon.

Continuing on into the mouth of the canyon, he ran into a trail that was concealed behind a large salt cedar. Once on the back side of the tree, the trail widened out until even a horse could easily pass over it.

As he looked up the trail, he could see puffs of smoke drifting toward him on the vagaries of the wind coming down the canyon. What was that from? It could be just some wanderer, a prospector, or anyone, and on the other hand, it could be an Indian, or an outlaw.

He stopped and searched the trail ahead closely with his eyes. The trail moved in and out, winding between salt cedar bushes, sagebrush and cactus. Grass and weeds created a mat on the canyon floor, and the empty creek bed followed closely by the twenty- foot-wide trail.

With every sense alert, Tom moved carefully up the loose-dirt pathway. The smoke smell grew stronger with each step he took.

Suddenly, the brush in the canyon ended and the bottom of the canyon was open for some distance. A water hole had been dug in the center of the clearing and a small fire was burning off to his right. A tarp had been erected on the same side of the canyon, and a corral was standing beyond the fire. A horse was tied to a post near the fire, and a man was trying to get a rope on the horse's back foot.

He was about to call out, but as the man bent over to tie the rope to the horse's foot, Tom could see a large US brand on the horse's hip. That was an Army horse!

Inching along, sometimes on his hands and knees, Tom scurried along the base of the wall to his left. He had to know if the horses in the corral were Army horses, as well. He kept watch on the man with the horse. When his back was turned Tom could move, otherwise, he had to lie flat and not attract the man's attention.

The man finally got the rope on the horse's leg, and pulled it up until the horse was standing on three legs. Tom watched as the man went to the fire and put some more wood on it. He then went to the tarp and came back with an iron. Tom couldn't tell for sure from that distance, but it looked to him like a branding iron. The man put one end of it into the fire, then, kneeled down and started making a cigarette. His back was to Tom, and it might be the best chance to make a run for it across the open area to the corral.

Running across the grassy area, Tom kept one eye on the man. In case he started to turn around, Tom could fall flat, and maybe not be seen. He made the corral undetected, and hunkered down behind the horses.

Two of them were unbranded, but there were eight Army horses in the bunch. They must have been stolen from the fort. The cavalry normally didn't sell any of their horses until they were too old, or too crippled, to serve their needs any more. These horses looked to be in prime condition.

Now what did he do? The man over there was between him and the mouth of the canyon. Tom was unarmed. He hadn't taken time to get his pistol before he left the fort. The man had a pistol and gunbelt on, and the holster was tied down. He very likely was adept with that gun. Unless the man would get really involved in some activity, Tom wouldn't be able to get by him and go for help. There wasn't much he could do, but see if he could find a place to get out of sight until the man left or was occupied.

He looked around and saw a large boulder that had fallen from the cliff at some past time. He waited until the man looked the other way and ran for it. As he reached the boulder, he threw himself flat on the ground, pressing every inch of his six-foot-four frame down into the sand.

He didn't get any reaction from the man, so he stayed hunkered down behind the big rock.

Peeking around the boulder, Tom watched the man brand the horse and then untie it and take it to the corral. As the man approached, Tom wondered if he was well enough hidden. The man opened the gate, led the horse through and removed the halter and hung it on a post. After he had closed the gate, he stood looking up the canyon. At times, Tom thought he was looking directly at him.

The man went back to the fire and picked up the branding iron and returned it to the tarp. Then he rolled another cigarette and sat by the tarp, leaned against a boulder, and sat smoking the cigarette. He was in no hurry and Tom was getting stiff from lying in one position behind that boulder.

The sun's rays disappeared suddenly as the sun sank behind the rim of the canyon. It was nearly dusk almost at once because of the narrow high walls of the canyon. The man threw some more wood on the fire and got out some pans and started making his supper. Tom could feel his belly crying for something to eat. It had been a long time since breakfast.

When the man had his meal cooked, he took it back to the tarp and sat eating his food. He finished and took his utensils down to the water hole and washed them. Tom had no option but to stay where he was and wait the man out. ·

As darkness settled in, the man unbuckled his gun belt and set it by his soogans, leaned his rifle against the pole the tarp was tied to, and went to bed.

After a while, Tom got to his feet. His legs were so stiff they would hardly hold him up, and the blood rushing to his feet about sent him crazy. He walked around a little to get his feet working properly again, and then made his way back toward the man's tarp. He was going to have to go by it to get out of the canyon.

Nearing the tarp, Tom walked as stealthily as he could. His scout training was coming in handy now. He saw the rifle standing there at the edge of the tarp, and he believed he could reach it if he could get just a little closer. The man appeared to be asleep.

He sneaked toward the tarp, taking every step slowly and carefully so as not to step on a twig or roll a rock under his foot. He got within reach of the gun and put his arm out to get the rifle. Just as he was about to wrap his hand around the barrel, the man grunted, and Tom jerked his hand back in reflex. The man made no more noise and Tom reached out once more for the weapon. This time he was able to grab it.

Now what? He could easily get on past the tarp now and out the canyon, but it probably was his duty to bring the man into the fort, and rescue the horses. He would have to have help to bring them in. He moved over in front of the tarp and pulled back the hammer of the rifle. He hoped the man had loaded the gun!

The man sat up. "What the h....?

"Just move slow. Raise your hands and crawl out of there. One move toward that pistol will be your last!"

"Who are you, and what are you doing here?"

"That really doesn't matter. Sit over there where I can watch you, and you can put on your boots. We're going for a walk."

As the man sat down and started to put his boots on, Tom squared around where he could keep the gun on the man, and at the same time reach in back of him for the man's pistol. Once he had that, he lay the rifle down and strapped the pistol to his waist. Then he picked the rifle up again. "All right, now get up and start for the mouth of the canyon. Go slow and no fast moves. My trigger finger is mighty itchy."

He could barely see the man as the firelight dwindled with every step on down the canyon. He kept the barrel of the rifle right in the man's back and his finger on the trigger.

Brush hit him in the face as they passed on down the trail. There was no way to see it in the dark, but he didn't dare hold up a hand to protect his face, for fear the outlaw would feel a slackening of pressure from the gun barrel and try to escape. When they reached the mouth of the canyon and came into the open prairie beyond it, the darkness lessened and he could make out the outline of the man pretty well.

Tom walked him down to where he had left his horse. The horse was gone. It probably headed back to the fort, after waiting so long for Tom's return. "Just head out that way." Tom pointed the barrel of the rifle in the direction of the fort. "Now move."

Daylight was starting over the horizon before Tom let the man sit down to rest. He didn't want the man to have a chance to try to get away until he could see every move he was making.

When it was light enough to see, the man looked at Tom. "You're a soldier! How did you find me? I didn't think any of you pony soldiers got that far away from your beds!"

"Sometimes we might surprise you. Who do you work for? I noticed the brand you put on the horse was the Box Eight. Who is the Box Eight? Where are they located?"

"Mister, save your breath. I'm not about to tell you. I don't know who owns it. I was hired in town and brought right out here. I don't know anything about the outfit. They bring the horses in to me. I work them and brand them, and later they come in after them. Every now and then, they pay me. The pay is good and I don't ask any questions."

"All right. We'll save that for later. Right now, get back on your feet and start walking again."

It was noon when the two men walked through the gates of the fort. Tom brought the man into Brewster's office and indicated a chair for him to sit in. He turned to the orderly. "Is the colonel in?"

"Yes, Sir. I'll let him know you're here."

Brewster came into the room. "Tom, where have you been? Gray Dove was looking for you last night, and this morning the horse you took came in without you. We were getting a search party together."

"Well, I took a ride, and this man took my interest. I think he's part of a horse-stealing outfit. He had some Army horses in a corral and was rebranding them. I thought you might like to talk to him."

"We've been losing a bunch of horses, and so have many of the other Army installations. You may have stumbled onto something."

Brewster called in the orderly. "Corporal, find the duty guard and bring him here. He may be eating; if so, tell him to postpone it. I want him to lock this man up." He turned back to Tom. "Good job, Lieutenant. Go find something to eat, and then I think your lady has been looking for you. I want to see you again at three. That's all."

Tom saluted and left the room.

From the entry room, he knocked on the Colonel's private door. Rosalyn answered. "Tom! You'd better throw in your hat. There is someone here that has been going crazy wondering where you are. I'll get her."

Gray Dove came back into the room with her. "Tom! Are you all right? I've been so worried. No one knew where you were."

"Well, I went out for an hour or so ride and ran into a rustler out there. I figured the Colonel would want to talk to him, so I waited until he was ready to travel."

"Well, the next time you run off for that long and don't tell me, you had better run, 'cause I'll pull out all of your hair!"

"Well, right now I think I'll go find something to eat. Want to walk over to the mess hall with me? I'll buy you a cup of coffee."

"All right."

At three o'clock, Tom walked into the colonel's office. "You wanted to see me, Sir?"

"Sit down, Tom. Tell me now how you found the rustler. I tried to interview him, but didn't get any information that was of any use. Where did you find him, and how many horses did he have?"

Tom told the colonel about the canyon, where it was located, and about the set-up they had there.

The colonel got up from his desk and paced around the room. "Tom, we aren't the only ones losing stock. Half the forts in this part of the country are in the same boat. Nobody seems to have any idea who is doing it, or how they are getting in to get the stock and then get them out without being seen. I think it's a big outfit, and they are obviously professionals.

"I have been giving this some thought since you were here at noon. I want you to get into your buckskins and go back to the canyon. They will be coming in with more horses, no doubt. Make out as if you stumbled into the canyon and saw that the stock weren't being fed, and then stayed to take care of them until somebody came back for them. Then ask for a job. If we can get someone inside their organization, maybe we can put a stop to the rustling of our horses."

"That might take some time. What about the reservation?"

"Do you trust Swensen to carry on what you started?"

"Yes. He can do just fine."

"All right then, this has to take priority as far as you are concerned. We've got to stop this loss of our horses now. We're having a real time trying to keep our troopers mounted, and the other forts are having the same trouble. This is the best opportunity we've had to get a handle on this, and I don't want to lose it. Get what supplies you need, and get back out there as soon as you can. Use your own horse. You don't dare go in there with a US brand.

"I'll contact Swensen and let him know it may be a time before you return. I'm sorry about your wedding plans, but you'll have to postpone that for a while. I'll try to explain to your bride-to-be the necessity for this."

"Yes, Sir, was there anything further?"

"That's it Tom. Use your own judgment as to what you need to do to get information on that gang, and how we can apprehend them. Get word to me when you can. You may need some funds. Pick them up out front. I'll have them ready for you in an hour. Good luck, Tom. You'll be on your own. There's not much way I can help you until you get the information we need."

Brewster held out his hand. Tom shook it, saluted, and left the room.

When he again knocked on the Colonel's private door, Rosalyn opened it. "Can't you leave that poor girl alone for more than five minutes?" Smiling, she turned. "I'll get her, and see if she'll see you."

Gray Dove came back with her. "Is something wrong, Tom?"

"Yes, the Colonel has a job for me that needs doing now. We will have to wait a little bit to get married. I hate to do that, but it seems I don't have any choice. I have to leave as soon as I can get my stuff together."

"How long will you be?"

"I don't know. He wants me to infiltrate a rustler bunch and get a handle on their operation. I can't say just how long that will take. I can't even let you know, because there isn't any way I can get in touch with you. It won't be any longer than I can help."

"All right, Tom. Then I think I will go back with Father. He is worrying that Maple Leaf is going to overdo. She has been working pretty hard on the cooking chores, and other things. Maybe I can help there. I'll be there when you get back. Take care of yourself." She put her arms around him and they kissed long and tenderly.

Darkness was settling fast when Tom pointed Dusty into the mouth of the canyon. When he reached the outlaw camp, he turned Dusty into the corral with the other horses, and then poured some of the rustlers' oats into the long feed box on one end of the corral. They had dug a trench in the far end of the corral where there was standing water which seeped from the underground creek. At least the horses had water while he was gone.

Tom built a fire, then, hauled out some jerky and biscuits from his saddle bags, ate, unrolled his soogans under the man's tarp, and went to sleep.

The next morning after he had eaten, he fed the horses, and then set out on foot to explore his surroundings. Once past the clearing where the outlaw camp was, the canyon narrowed. Once again it was filled with trees and brush. This time there were some pine trees, sage and rabbit brush, as well as juniper. The trail continued on through the timber, and Tom followed it. He might want to know where it went if he ran into trouble with the gang.

The canyon bottom continued to rise, and the vertical walls grew shorter. Now there was a running stream coursing down the canyon bottom. A little further on, the stream ended. It appeared to flow out from under the cliff on the left side of the canyon. Tom lay down and drank deeply. The water was clear and cold.

After another half an hour's hike, the trail topped out onto the mesa that ran along the top of the canyon on both sides. The mesa extended along the top of the vertical cliff that he had followed coming from the fort. It extended to his right as far as he could see. At least it was a route he could take if he had to get away. He returned to camp.

The next two days were spent taking care of the horses, and exploring around his camp. The third day was cloudy, and Tom thought it might bring up a storm. He made breakfast, took care of the horses, and returned to the tarp. He had seen most of the surrounding countryside and thought he would just hang around camp today.

About midday he heard some horses coming up the canyon. He left the tarp and walked over to the side of the canyon and stood behind a tree. Two men came in leading four horses each. The ones he could see each had a US brand on the back right hip. Tom stepped out where he could be seen. The man in front made a grab for his pistol, but Tom had his out before he could get it done. "Just rest easy. And dismount on this side of your horse."

"Who are you and what are you doing here? Where's Jason?"

"I don't know who Jason is. I haven't seen anybody. Now if we can be friends, I'll go open that corral gate for you."

"You've got the drop. Go ahead."

After they had the horses in the corral, and the ridden horses unsaddled, they walked back over to the fire.

The lead man turned to Tom, his hand near his gun. "Now, mister, I want to know who you are, where Jason is, and what you're doing here."

"Well, I could say the same about you, but I got nothing to hide. My name is Bill Gooding. Just up from Texas. I'm just drifting through, and looking for a grubstake for the winter."

"How did you get in here? This isn't easy to find."

"Well, I didn't try to find it. I was riding along the rim down there and it looked like a storm coming up. I saw the canyon and thought I could go in there and get out of the storm. When I got in here I saw this camp, and the horses in the corral looked like they could use a feed, so I fed them. I haven't seen this Jason, or anybody."

The man studied him a long time. "I wonder where in the blue side of hell he is. His horse is in the corral. Mister, I don't know whether to trust you, or not. I guess we can get something to eat and I'll think about it. Maybe Jason will be back by then. Name's Bartlett. That there's Fortner."

They foraged around under the tarp, found a pot and some hardtack and the makings for a stew. When it was hot, they loaded up some tin plates that were in Jason's supplies and sat down by the fire to eat.

Tom kept his gun side toward the other two. He watched them as they ate. Bartlett was a large man. He had thinning hair, bushy eyebrows and a wide, prominent mouth. His hands were thick, and Tom thought, powerful. The muscles in his shoulders stretched the fabric of his shirt to the popping point. Fortner was just the opposite. He was pencil thin, with bones protruding almost through his skin in many places. His eyes were narrow slits in his face and he had a small, thin-lipped mouth. Tom thought neither one were the type he would like to meet on a dark night in a back alley.

When they had finished eating and their plates had been cleaned off at the water hole, Bartlett sat by the fire rolling a cigarette. "So, Gooding, you're travelin' through. Where to?"

"About wherever my horse takes me. I'm sorta between jobs right now."

"You from Texas? You sorta sound like it."

"Yep. About a hundred miles east of El Paso. I worked for the Rafter R. Man by the name of Roberts owned it. Summer work was about over, so I drifted."

"I've been in El Paso several times. I never heard of the Rafter R."

"It was a pretty small outfit. Only two of us besides the old man."

"You're lookin' for work, you say?"

"Only enough to build a grubstake for the winter."

"Well, if you want to help us rebrand these horses we bought from the Army, you can come with us. Maybe the boss'll take you on for the winter."

"You bought them from the Army? I didn't know they ever sold 'em."

"Yeah, when they get so old they get rid of 'em. We can rebrand them and sell them to city slickers, or small farmers, and make a little profit. Sometimes the liveries will take them for rental horses."

The next morning after they had eaten, they got a branding fire going, and Bartlett picked the Box Eight iron out from under the tarp and laid it in some coals.

"Gooding, you keep the iron hot, and Fortner and I will get the horses in the chute and brand 'em."

Tom almost asked why Jason didn't use the chute to brand the horse, but caught himself in time. He still wondered why.

The branding took the rest of the morning. Tom was amazed at how neatly the Box Eight brand fit right over the US brand. It was a snap. All of the Army branding irons were the same size. All the rustlers had to do was measure one US brand, forge an iron that matched it in size but change it to a Box Eight, and the new brands look like an original.

When they had finished, Bartlett took the iron out of the fire and started back for the tarp. "Good, we'll eat just before dark and start out."

Tom asked, "You're going to drive 'em after dark?"

"Yeah, its cooler then, and we like to push the herd pretty fast. They won't get so het up that way. Get your gear together and be ready to move."

At dusk, after they had eaten, Bartlett opened the corral gate and ran the horses out into the open area. "Fortner, get out to the mouth of the canyon and get 'em turned left. Gooding, you and I'll chouse 'em on out."

They soon had the horses lined out down the trail, and before long they were in the open, out of the canyon. They turned the herd to the left, and Bartlett and Fortner each took one side and left the drag for Tom to handle.

Tom tried to keep track of the direction they were traveling, but the night was cloudy and he could only get an occasional look at the stars. It seemed to him that it was generally in a northern direction that they were traveling.

A dim gray light was starting to form when Bartlett pulled in behind a grove of trees. There was a corral there, well hidden from any passing traveler. He opened the gate, and they pushed the horses inside.

As Bartlett closed the gate, Tom said, "You men have this pretty well organized. You must have been at it for a while."

"Yeah, the boss has things lined out pretty well. He didn't build up the Box Eight because he was some kind of dummy."

"How did he get started, anyway?"

"Mister, you ask a lot of questions. You'd be a lot better off to keep 'em to yourself."

"Sorry. I was just impressed with how smoothly your outfit worked."

Again, they waited out the day, and with the advent of darkness, once more took to the trail. This night the stars were out, and Tom could come closer to making out the direction they were traveling. It definitely was a northerly heading. The two outlaws kept the band pretty well bunched, and Tom kept them moving.

The next morning, Bartlett didn't stop them when daylight burst forth, but kept the horses moving at a fast pace.

About mid-morning, they topped a bare ridge and Tom could see a ranch down below. It appeared to be fairly good size. The ranch house was on the sidehill above the shallow valley, with the barn below it and several smaller sheds in between. One of them probably was the bunkhouse. A corral was to one side of the barn. Bartlett rode ahead to open the corral gate and they drove the horses in and closed the gate.

Bartlett pointed to the bunkhouse. "Tie your horse to the hitchrack for now and find an empty bunk in there. I'll go see if the boss is here. Fortner, come with me."

Tom took his gear into the bunkhouse and laid it on an empty bunk. He looked around the room. It looked as if there were only four of the eight bunks being occupied. That wasn't much of a crew for what appeared to be a big ranch. The ranch house and barn were both large, and obviously expensive. He walked back out and took Dusty to the water trough for a well-earned drink. He loosened the saddle cinch, then, stood looking over the countryside.

Presently, Bartlett and Fortner came back out of the ranch house and down to where Tom was standing. "The foreman says to hang up your hat. You're on the payroll, for a while anyway. Supper's at six in that left wing of the ranch house, breakfast at six, as well. Lunch is when you can get it. Put your saddle in the tack room in the barn and your horse in the corral. You're on your own until supper. The foreman will lay out tomorrow's work then." The two went on into the bunkhouse.

It was still a couple of hours until supper. Tom decided to walk around the farmstead and get the lay of the land as best he could. You never knew when it might come in handy. He looked around the barn. It was a large hip-roof building. It had stalls on the ground floor, a tack room, and there was an alley that went down the middle to a double back door. Tom could see hay in the loft through the manhole cut in the floor. A ladder reached up to the manhole. At the back of the building, a fence stretched from the double doors to the corral, with a gate just outside the door that led to the holding pasture beyond. A really nice setup.

If he took a detour from the barn to the creek running just beyond the ranch house, it would keep him from prying eyes in the house, and still give him a chance to see that part of the farmstead. Skirting the area near the house, he arrived at the creek. He found some shade and sat watching the water, trying to collect his thoughts.

He knew that he was skating on thin ice. One slip with this bunch and it would be his last. Bartlett had been suspicious of him from the start.

Tracks around the corral showed that this wasn't the first bunch of horses that had gone through there. Of course there was no way of knowing if they were Army horses or not now, but he'd bet they were. The Army remuda was about the same mix of older horses and barely broke green ones. All of them had the U S brand on the right hip. All of them, that is, except those with the altered Box Eight brand.

He stayed down by the creek until supper time, then walked back to the water trough and washed up. Then he made his way to the ranch house and entered the building.

There was a large stove and counter on the far end of the room. Cupboards were on the wall to either side of the stove. A long table went down the center of the room with wooden benches on either side. Plates and silverware were already in place.

Bartlett and Fortner were seated at the far end of the table, and just as Tom stepped into the room, four cowboys came in behind him. Tom took a seat at the far end of the table, and the four cowboys sat on the bench across from him.

A man as big as Bartlett came in and sat across from Bartlett and Fortner. They talked for some time in low tones so that what they said was not distinguishable to Tom. Soon the meal was on the table and talk was sporadic. Tom listened to the talk of the cowboys, and as near as he could tell, it was the same as cowboy talk anywhere - mostly weather, cows, and Saturday night.

After Tom had eaten, he started to rise, and the man across from Bartlett stood up and looked over at Tom. "Gooding, before you go to your bunk, I want you to come with me."

Tom walked over to where the man was standing. He stood a couple of inches taller than Tom, and he was as about as wide as he was tall. He had eyebrows an inch thick over steel-hard eyes gleaming beneath them. He sported a large, thin nose and pencil-thin lips over a jutting jaw. "Bartlett tells me you want to hire on."

"Just for the winter."

CHAPTER FOURTEEN

Frost was on Ole's blanket when he woke up. They were going to get the Agency building done just in time. The soldiers were all still sleeping down by the fires, but it was going to be downright miserable if he didn't get them inside pretty soon.

Ole got dressed and walked down to the main fire. It was already going, and he could get a cup of coffee down there. Sergeant Bascomb was sitting on a rock by the fire when Ole got there. Ole poured himself a cup of coffee and sat down beside him.

"Sergeant, how is the Agency building coming? Vill ve get in today? Clouds have been rolling in ewery day, and I t'ink ve're going to be in for a storm wery soon."

"Yes, Sir, I think we'll be in today. We put the big stove in yesterday, and the doors are built and we'll hang them today. Then we should be ready for the troops. We have enough families into the new teepees that everyone will have a heated space to sleep in now. We moved the men from the barn to the warehouse two days ago."

"Good vork."

Ole went back to his wagon. He'd move his gear to the Agency building today. Pretty Rose should be along soon. He didn't know what he would do without her. She filled in when Gray Dove left, and she was his only means of talking to the Indians. Besides that, she was pretty and smart, and he liked being with her.

Today was the big meeting with the tribal council. They were unhappy that the men and wives had to sleep apart so long. There just wasn't any way they could give them privacy until they could get teepees for all of them. He had hunters out every day trying to get hides for new teepees, but there was only so much they could do. Besides that, the smoke house was almost full. He wished that Tom was here. He'd know what to tell the council. If the chief was here, he would take care of it. Boy, this being an agent wasn't any fun.

Pretty Rose came in with Gray Dove's list of families. Ole poured her a cup of coffee and they sat down on the bench he'd had Bascomb make and started going over the lists.

Pretty Rose pointed to the names that had a mark beside them. "These are the families that have received teepees. The others are still sleeping in the tribal building and the warehouse."

Ole took the list. There were nearly half of the families that still didn't have their teepees. It was going to be a long winter. At least he'd have them in heated buildings when the cold weather hit.

As he was going over the list he couldn't help feeling Pretty Rose's presence sitting next to him. He went over the list a couple of times, not wanting to break the spell. "Pretty Rose, the last agent used to valk vith his interpreter down by the creek in the ewening. Ay t'ink ve should keep up the tradition. Vat do you t'ink?"

She smiled at him. "I would not want to break such a tradition."

Ole returned the smile. "Vell, then, let's go talk to the council, and ve can extend traditions tonight if the council doesn't kill us."

Pretty Rose looked at him mischievously. "I t'ink ve should."

One after another the council members got up and talked extensively. Pretty Rose tried to keep up with their speech and at the same time interpret it for Ole. Some hours after the sun had hit its zenith, the tribal portion of the meeting finally ended.

Ole stood up. "Ay understand your feelings. Your people vould like to bring their families back together. Ve are bringing hides in as fast as ve can, v'ile still taking care of the meat from the animals ve already killed. Ve vill put them in their own homes as fast as ve can."

Pretty Rose interpreted his words to the council, and then sat down. The councilmen talked among themselves for a time, and then the leader stood, followed by the others, and they left the teepee.

Ole turned to Pretty Rose. "Vat did they say?"

"They were still unhappy, but said they would talk to the chief when he returns."

Walking hand in hand down the path to the creek, Ole led Pretty Rose to Tom and Gray Dove's favorite spot. He helped her down to a seat in front of the big pine, and then sat beside her. He put an arm around her and they leaned back against the tree.

"Ay have vanted to ask you to come down here vith me for a long time. Ay'm glad you said yes."

"I'm glad you asked me."

Moving into the Agency building took up the next day, and Ole soon realized that there was a real need to separate a room for all the business papers and other paraphernalia that had accumulated, and a place where he could talk to the soldiers and Indians without having to do so in the same room where the soldiers were barracked. He needed a place for privacy talks as much as the chief did.

He instructed Bascomb to have the crew build one, and to put a room with it for the Agent's quarters. It would have to be the Agency office for some time probably. He also requested a separate outside door to the office. The Indians might not want to walk in to the room where the soldiers were billeted to take their troubles to him.

How was Tom going to feel about the changes? Well, he had left him in charge – he'd just have to live with it.

Two more weeks went by. He was looking forward to his nightly walks with Pretty Rose. She had started calling him Ole now, and he was calling her just Pretty. They were getting mighty close, he thought. She was in his thoughts often, every day.

Everything was going according to schedule, he reckoned. Tom should be pleased with the progress.

Ole looked up from the pile of papers he had been working on. There was a knock on his outside door. Probably an Indian that needed an extra ration tonight. Several had come down with some stomach problem, and Maple Leaf had been tending to them. He laid the papers down and walked over and opened the door.

"Sergeant Draper reporting, Sir."

"Sergeant, you aren't from our troop. Vere are you from?"

"From the fort, Sir. We were detailed to bring Chief Capture and his daughter back to the reservation.

"Vere are they now?"

The sergeant handed a sheaf of papers to Ole. "The daughter said she would be over to see you as soon as she got her father settled. These are dispatches that Colonel Brewster said to deliver to you. With your permission, I'll go see to my men now."

"Permission granted, Sergeant. And thank you."

Ole went back to shuffling papers. He'd get even with Tom one of these days. This was no job for a wild frontiersman. He needed a desk to make notes on. Writing on his knee was for the birds. He'd have to tell Bascomb to put one of the crews to work on it.

There was a knock on the door and Gray Dove walked in. "Hello, Ole. I just wanted to let you know we are back. My father said to ask you if you could meet with him when you have time."

"Hello, Gray Dove. It's good to see you. Vere's Tom?"

"The colonel's got him off on some sort of investigation. I don't know what it's all about, but Tom said he might be a while."

"Dang! Ay vas about to hand this yob back to him and go hunting, or somet'ing. Vell, Ay'm glad you're back. How did the trial go?"

"They declared him innocent, or whatever they call it in the Army. He is free. He said to tell you to keep on with what you're doing."

"Thanks for the news. Tell your father Ay vill be ower shortly."

"All right, Ole. I'll see you then." She left, and Ole sat digesting what she had told him.

Pretty Rose rapped on the pole and entered the teepee. "I heard you were back. Not even coming to see me?"

"You know better than that. I was just getting my father settled first. Have you got time for a walk?"

"All right, let's go."

They walked in silence down to the creek and sat down under the favorite pine tree. Pretty Rose put her hand on Gray Dove's arm. "I've missed you. I'm glad you're back. Where's Tom?"

"The colonel has him on some kind of mission. I don't know when he'll be back. Oh, Pretty, I'm so confused. Tom asked me to marry him. We were all ready for the ceremony when Tom had to leave. The fort women were all very nice, and I like Rosalyn, the colonel's wife, really well, but I just felt out of place."

"Well, you'll be out here with us after you're married. What difference does all that make?"

"What if he gets transferred, or something?"

"Why worry about that? You'll be with him. That's all that counts."

"You are a peach. I can always count on you to make things seem all right."

"Well, you won't think so when I tell you that I have stolen your favorite sparking place. Ole and I have been coming down here every night. You and Tom are just going to have to find another one."

"Oh, Pretty, I'm so glad. I like Ole." She gave Pretty a big hug. "I was afraid you would be an old woman without a husband because no man was good enough for you!" She smiled and hugged her friend again.

Looking across the room at Master Sergeant Bull Bascomb, Ole wondered how he ever go along without him. All you had to do was ask and Bascomb figured a way to get done whatever you wanted. He was a jewel among jewels. He had honed the tribal police into a unit that any city would be proud to have. Buildings were getting built as fast as a man could ask for. And the Indians were getting to be accepting of their fate, and now working toward making a life for themselves.

Tom had set the tone for the reservation, and all Ole had to do was keep it going. He had to admit there were humps and bumps along the way, but he was getting the hang of how to solve the problems when a solution was available.

Pretty was the joy of his life. She solved his problems when an interpretation was needed, and often took care of it herself if she could. He was growing more in love with her every day. Life just wasn't all bad. He was going to be just a little reluctant to turn the reins back over to Tom when he got back. He was starting to enjoy it—for the most part anyhow, and he sensed the Indians were starting to like him.

CHAPTER FIFTEEN

"I'm Jeb Barker. I ramrod this outfit. We can use another hand. Rusty, come over here."

One of the cowboys that had been sitting across from Tom walked over. Barker waved a thumb at Tom. "This's a new hand. Takin' Reno's place. Take him along with your crew tomorrow."

Rusty stuck out his hand. "Rusty Mitchell. Glad to have you. We can use another hand. Come on. We'll palaver down at the bunkhouse."

"Bill Gooding."

Tom followed Rusty out of the building and down to the bunkhouse. Rusty took a seat on his bunk, and Tom sat on his. Rusty said. "Where are you from?"

"Texas."

"I came from Oklahoma territory last year. You've worked cattle?"

"Some. I was on the Rafter R down there for a while."

"Well, glad to have you. You lucked out. We have a pretty good crew working the cattle. The horse punchers are a pretty tough bunch. Barker pretty much leaves us alone. He sticks pretty close with the horse crew."

Just then the other three cowboys walked in. Rusty pointed to Tom. "Fellers, this is Bill Gooding. He's goin' to be workin' with us. Bill, this ugly galoot here is Casey, this is Red, and the shy one over there is Phil." They all shook hands and exchanged pleasantries for a time.

Eating quickly, then saddling their horses and riding out to the herd went as it would on any ranch Tom had ever been on. They moved cattle from one pasture to another to take them to grass that hadn't yet been grazed.

The first two days were spent building fence, and the third day they moved some yearlings to the steer pasture. How in heck was he going to get any information on the operation working here with these cowboys? It was just like working on any cow ranch, and the others were off somewhere catching government horses. He had to do something.

That night after supper, he caught Jeb Barker just after he had finished eating. "Mr. Barker, I'm thinking I'm not going to get my stake earned by the time winter sets in. I'm pretty fair at bronc-busting. How would you go for a deal? I'll top out all the horses you bring in for ten dollars each. Then when you sell them, you can sell them as well-broke ponies, even for women and children."

"Most buyers can break their own. Not many men can't break their own, too. Pretty good are you?"

"Above average."

"All right, I'll think on it. Let you know in the morning."

The next morning after breakfast, Barker cornered Tom. "Stay in this morning. We've got a few salty ones down in the corral. Let's see what you can do."

They had a horse snubbed to the post in the middle of the corral when Tom got there with his saddle. It was a buckskin, with a roman nose and a wild look in his eyes. It stomped and snorted and tried to get loose from the rope. Tom walked around behind him when he came up with the saddle. It wasn't an Army horse. It had a brand Tom didn't recognize.

Sitting on the top rail of the corral were Jeb Barker and half a dozen other men. Tom could see that they came to watch the show. This was a ringer! They had brought in an outlaw horse that probably few could ride, and they were going to test him. Well, he'd try to be ready for him.

Tom cinched on the saddle till it was good and tight, got the bridle on, and then he stood by the horse's head. He petted him on his nose and rubbed his mane a little to try to calm him down. Then he looped the reins up, cinched down on them, grabbed the horn and got a foot in a stirrup, then swung aboard.

The buckskin stood a moment, and then all heck broke loose. The horse unwound quickly, jumping up to the right, weaving in the air and coming down to the left. Each landing was stiff-legged, jolting Tom's back every time. It felt with every jump like the horse had a belly full of bedsprings. Tom kept a tight hold on the reins trying to keep the horse's head up, but not always successfully.

When the horse couldn't unseat Tom, it started to sunfish. Jumping high off the ground, twisting and turning while it was in the air, and then landing stiff legged with a jarring impact. Tom had to pull leather a time or two to keep his seat.

Finally the horse tired, made a few crow-hops, and then cantered around the corral. Tom rode him over to the post and tied him, removed his saddle and bridle and turned the horse loose.

Barker jumped down off the fence and walked over to where Tom was throwing his saddle over the railing. "That was a good ride, Gooding. You've got a job. None of us was able to stick on him."

"Where are the ones you want tamed?"

"There in the holding pasture. Pick out which ones you want to start with. They all need to be ridden. You can set your own schedule."

"Thanks, I'll start after I get a few muscles straightened out."

Getting out of bed the next couple of days was painful. It took until after breakfast each day to get the kinks out of his legs until he could walk easily again. He picked out the horses that he felt would be the toughest to gentle and rode them first.

After the first few days, all of the worst ones had been ridden at least once. Then he started to ride out several of the tame ones and then each day, he rode a bad one once more, just to keep him aware that he was supposed to be a riding horse.

After two weeks of breaking horses, Tom still had no inkling of what was happening with the horse rustlers. He would see them go to the ranch house in a bunch and then saddle up and ride off. They didn't bring in any more Army horses, or any other kind. Were they through for the year? It was starting to get cool nights, and fall was half over. It would be winter soon and he hadn't accomplished much of anything as far as getting information on the rustlers was concerned.

He built a loop and dropped it over the head of a buckskin that was about the hardest of the bunch to train. Every day he climbed on him it was a battle, until he got all of the buck out of him. Once he settled down, he was a really good horse. He had a lot of bottom. Tom had taken him out one day and run him for hours, and he still had go left in him when Tom was worn out. Tom had named him Ornery.

Deciding that one way or another he was going to wear that horse down, Tom took to riding him twice a day, in between working with the other horses. He developed a real affection for the horse, and before long, it was being returned. The horse would nicker and come to Tom when he entered the corral, but he would still buck like crazy for a short time when Tom got on him. The bucking time did start to get shorter every day, however.

The sun was just going down over the horizon. Tom wearily tied the last horse to the post and removed his saddle and bridle and the blanket and draped them all over the top rail. He was bushed! A couple of them had given him a pretty good ride this day!

As he approached the bunkhouse Jeb Barker hollered at him. "Gooding, wait a minute. You've about got these whipped into shape. We've got another bunch coming in a couple of days and need to get these to market. I lost a couple of my herders last week and I want you to help herd these. We'll start early in the morning."

"One thing: I want to buy that buckskin from you."

"You want that one? I've seen you fighting with him about every day. Why would you want him?"

"I guess it's just that I want to see if I can ever get the best of him."

"You can have him. I don't think I could sell him to anyone, anyhow."

"Thanks. I'll be ready in the morning."

The outlaws that had jumped him back at the canyon were there with two others at breakfast the next morning. There was no conversation with Tom, but they talked together occasionally. Trying his best to hear their conversation, all he could catch were brief snatches of their talk once in a while. It was obvious they still didn't trust him completely.

When he had finished eating, Tom saddled Dusty and put a lead-rope on Ornery, then, waited for the others to get ready to go. Once they had saddled their horses, they opened the corral gate, and the drive was on.

It was at the end of a long two-day drive when Jeb reined down from a ridge into a farmstead similar to the one they had left. There was a large wooden sign over the gate to the yard reading Box Eight. This was the other farm the company owned. They put the horses in the corral by the barn and then they all walked up to the ranch house.

It was obvious that the crews of the two ranches knew each other well. Tom walked over to a chair by the wall and sat down. He watched the crews get reacquainted, and tried to listen to their conversations, hoping he might gain some information. About all he could pick up was that they were planning a drive the next morning. Were they finally going to get to their buyer, so he could bring some kind of information back to the colonel? He'd like to get this assignment done, so he wouldn't have to be on edge all the time, watching every move he made or what he said.

They were called to supper shortly after that, and when they had eaten, Tom went to the barn, untied his soogans and went to sleep.

They rolled him out early the next morning for breakfast, and then turned the horses they had driven in, along with another bunch about as big, out of the corral, and they started the trek, to where Tom had no idea.

Three more days' travel brought them to the outskirts of Kansas City. They put the horses in a large corral at the edge of town. When the horses were all inside the corral, Jeb Barker said. "There's a ten-dollar bonus for each of you. I'll be over by the building there. Come by and I'll give you the bonus and your wages. Go have a good time tonight, but not so good a time that you can't ride back home first thing in the morning."

After they were paid, the whole crew made a bee-line for the nearest saloon. Tom held back, and Bartlett saw him standing there watching them go. He came back. "What's the matter, Gooding? Are you too good to drink with the rest of us?"

"I'll be along later. I have a friend that used to live here. I'm going to see if I can find him."

"Just be sure you're back here in time to leave in the morning."

"I'll be here."

Tom waited until they were out of sight, then circled the block to his right to be sure nobody was watching, then returned to where he could watch the corral without being seen.

Barker and the manager of the second ranch sat on their horses talking for some time. It appeared that they were having a difference of opinion about something. Finally they left together, and Tom followed them to a nearby hotel. Tom watched for some time but they didn't come back out of the building. He was about to get his horse when they came out the door with a third man. They walked down the boardwalk to a restaurant a couple of blocks down the street.

Tom followed. That third man must be the buyer. He was a smaller man than the other two, but Tom couldn't make out any features from the back. He was going to have to get a better look at the man if he was going to bring Brewster any useful information. Of course, he didn't know this was the buyer, but it was his guess that it was.

Walking up to the covered porch on the restaurant, Tom inched along the wall, trying to get to a spot where he could get a look at the stranger. Looking through the first window he came to, he could see that they weren't in that end of the room. They must have gone on to the other end. He crossed in front of the door, and edged along the wall toward the other window.

He could see Barker and the other foreman sitting at a table facing his direction. The stranger was sitting across from them with his back toward Tom. Damn the luck! How was he going to find out who he was? He tried to inch a little further down the wall where maybe he could get a side view of the man anyhow.

Just then, two of the herders he had come with came up behind him. "Hey, Gooding, what are you doing?"

Tom turned back to them. "Just trying to see if the steaks looked any good."

"Well, come on in. Let's find out."

Tom didn't see any way out so he followed them into the building. He tried to keep the others between Barker's group and himself. Fortner saw Barker sitting there and started over toward him.

Tom said, "Go ahead. I'm going to get something to eat." He sat with his back toward Barker's group, hoping that he wouldn't get called over there.

Mitchell, Fortner's compadre, sat down with Tom. "Me, too. I'm starved." Fortner changed his mind and sat down again. Tom was glad. At least this way, he didn't stand out so much.

Watching covertly out of the corner of his eye, Tom could see Barker and the foreman of the other ranch talking earnestly with the stranger. Then he thought that he could see money change hands from the stranger to the two foremen. Was this the big boss? What was the money for? Tom watched more closely. No bill of sale was passed over. Was it handled at a previous time, or was it just payroll for the hands?

The three men apparently concluded their business and stood up. Barker stopped at their table "Back to the ranch in the morning. I'll meet you in the lobby of the Mountain View hotel at eight sharp."

The other two walked straight from their table out the door, and Tom couldn't get a good look at the stranger. He had a hat on and his collar turned up as if he didn't want to be seen. That was logical, Tom thought, buying stolen horses, if that is what he was doing. Barker walked over and paid his bill and followed the other two.

Tom got up. "I think I'm going to skip supper. I'll see you in the morning. I've got to try to see my friend tonight if I can."

Mitchell grinned. "She must be a very good friend if you're goin' to skip a meal just to see her."

"Pretty good."

He hurried out the door, and could just see the three down the sidewalk, headed to the hotel. They entered the building and disappeared. Tom waited and watched outside for some time, but they did not reappear.

Giving up on seeing them again this night, Tom went back to his horses and rode up to the livery. As he pulled up to the door, he noticed that it was only a short distance to the corrals where they had put the horses. Good! He could watch in the morning to see what happened to them. He took the horses inside and the man stabled them. Tom made arrangements to sleep in the hayloft overnight.

The next morning, just as daylight was settling in, Tom walked over to the corral. He found a leafy bush nearby and sat down on the grass behind it in a place where he had a view of the corral.

Hunger began eating at him, and he had about made up his mind to go get something to eat when a small group of soldiers entered the corral. He recognized a couple of them from the fort. It was tempting to say hello to them, but he decided to wait and see what was happening. Soon, the stranger from the café walked into the corral. What did he have to do with the soldiers? Tom wished that he was closer. He'd like to get a better look at that man. The hat and long coat covered him really well.

The man turned Tom's way as he was talking to a soldier. The soldier was directly in front of him so that Tom couldn't get a good view, but there was something familiar about him. The way he stood, or gestured, or something. Tom just couldn't put a finger on it. Then the soldier stepped away. Fister! That was Fister standing there! Was he on a legitimate buying expedition for the fort, or was this a nefarious scheme on his part? How was he going to find out?

He had no proof that Fister knew the horses were stolen, but guessed he would take what he knew to Brewster. He walked back away from the corral, keeping out of sight, and taking a back alley, went to the hotel. It was half-past eight and he wondered if Barker was still there.

Barker and the other foreman were sitting in two chairs at one side of the lobby when Tom entered the hotel. Barker looked up. "You're late, Gooding. I said eight sharp. You're lucky a couple of the others are late, too, or I'd have been gone. I should take a late fee out of your salary. The others are at the corral. I'll see you back at the ranch."

"No, I'm taking my time. I said I would work until I had a stake for the winter. This'll last me with what I already have. How much did you get for the bunch? I thought we'd get a bigger bonus, or something, for bringing in that herd."

"It's none of your business, and you get your wages just like the rest of us. Besides, you did get the mustang out of the deal."

Well, Tom thought, that about shows that Fister owns the two ranches, and is paying these guys just wages, and keeping the profit.

What a sweet deal, and he is the buyer for the Army. He can set the sale price and then put on his soldier cap and agree to it.

"I thank you for the job, and I'll be on my way. May see you again if I get hard up for cash."

"All right, Gooding. I hate to see you go. You did a good job with those mustangs. If you need a job sometime, come back."

Tom crossed the lobby and went out the front door. He saw Fister coming down the street and he ducked into the alley beside the hotel. No use letting Fister know he'd been spotted. It might be easier to prove his misdeeds if he wasn't aware he had been seen.

Four days' hard riding brought him in sight of the fort. He rode in and put his horses in the corral, then went to his quarters and washed up before reporting to Brewster.

Colonel Brewster was sitting behind his desk when Tom was ushered in by the orderly. "Tom, good to see you! Did you find out who's been stealing our horses? It's been so long that I began to wonder if you had run into some trouble."

"Nothing I couldn't handle, Sir." Tom told the colonel the details of the trip, gave him the names of the miscreants, and told him of the Box Eight over-brand.

"That's clever. I wonder how many Box Eight horses we have purchased?"

"I checked the corral when I put my horse away. Over half of them are Box Eight."

"I'm going to have to warn Fister to look out for them. We are buying our own horses back!"

"Yes, Sir, we are, but I don't think you have to warn Fister. I'm sure he owns the Box Eight ranches where the stolen horses are being taken. He hires the men who steal them, and then buys them back for the Army."

"That's hard to believe, Tom! Have you any proof?"

"Only that I worked for the outfit, and watched the stolen horses being re-branded. I saw Fister hand over the money to the thieves and pick the horses up the next morning to bring them here. I'd suggest that you ask him for the bill of sale for the horses when he brings them in. He won't have one.

"Also, he will be bringing in a bay with three white stockings and a star on his forehead, that many of the troopers here will recognize. There are several others that can verify that Fister is the boss. Barker is the foreman on one of his ranches, a man named Bartlett, and one named Fortner, work for him. All of them know Fister. Fortner would be a good one to question. He's a pretty weak man, and would come clean without a lot of questioning, I think."

"Well, Tom, these are serious charges. It pains me that one of my men would stoop so low. I'll take him into custody when he gets here with the horses. If I can't get him to confess, you may have to be available for the trial."

"I hope that he does. I'm anxious to get back to the reservation."

Brewster smiled. "She'll be waiting, but I have to tell you that you aren't going back to the reservation, Captain. The agent we have there is doing such a good job that I'm going to leave him there. The Indians all like him, and everything is running smoothly, so why rock the boat?"

"What do you mean, 'Captain'? And why won't I be going back?"

"Colin Borden, my adjutant, has been pulled back to serve on the general's staff. He apparently made a hit with the general when he was out here. I asked to have you assigned to replace him. The rank carries a captain's bars. Congratulations, Tom! I'm looking forward to working with you. I need a man I can trust completely in that job."

"I appreciate your confidence, Sir, but I'm a field man. All of my experience has been in the field. I'd be clear out of my element. I wouldn't know what I was doing!"

"Tom, all of my early training was in the East. My trail up through the ranks was guarding army facilities, fighting in the war, and on the general's staff. They then sent me out here as adjutant for Cal Armand. When he retired they appointed me to this job. I've been here ever since. I need someone with your experience in the field, especially along the lines of establishing reservations.

"As a matter of fact there is another group of Sioux in the compound now that will be requiring your attention shortly. There aren't quite enough yet to make up another reservation, but we have patrols out now, working at rounding up a few more. Your first job will be to organize a crew to set up the next reservation. You can give them first-hand knowledge as to how to go about it. The Army has had no experience along those lines, and there is going to be a lot of that in the future. And Tom, in any but formal situations, I am Charley to you."

"Thank you, Sir - er, Charley. When do I start the new job?"

"You're in it. You have been since shortly after you left."

"Would it be possible to have a couple of weeks' vacation before I get up to my elbows in the new job?"

Brewster smiled and handed Tom a sheaf of papers. "I'm way ahead of you. I knew you would have to see that girl of yours first. You are due in your office two weeks from today at 8:00 AM sharp. However, I expect to see you here two days before that. Rosalyn has a dress about finished and needs someone to wear it, and the chaplain will be ready to perform the ceremony. Now get on your horse and I don't want to see you before that." He grinned and slapped Tom on the back.

Tom stopped on the ridge above the valley. It was a funny feeling looking down on that scene. The first time he did that it was an open grassy valley between two hills, and he was leading three hundred Indians that he had to do something with, and quick. Now, his dreams had come true. Cattle in the corral and a barn half full of hay, a tribal building, a warehouse and now even an Agency building! Teepees were lined up on both sides of the valley. It really was a great feeling of accomplishment. He nudged the horse into motion and rode down into the village.

He knocked on the teepee door pole and Gray Dove herself opened the flap. When she saw Tom she flew into his arms. "Oh, Tom, I've missed you! Where have you been all this time?" She threw her arms around his neck and kissed him.

"I'll tell you all about it tonight. I've got several things that I need to do yet today. And the daylight is running out. Are you all right? Did you have a good trip coming back?

She smiled. "Yes, yes and yes". Then she grew serious. "I'll see you tonight."

"I need to talk to your father. Will you interpret?"

"Of course."

Tom entered the teepee and shook Chief Capture's hand. "Chief, Colonel Brewster sends his regards. He hopes you had a good trip back. He also wanted to thank you for your testimony at the trial. I want to thank you again, also. I might still be in jail if you hadn't testified."

Gray Dove translated the message, and the Chief and Tom talked for some time with Gray Dove translating for both of them. Finally, Tom said, "I've got to see Ole. Will he be in the agency building?"

"Yes, you can usually find him there this time of day."

Tom took his leave, and walked over to the Agency building, and walked in. Bascomb and several soldiers were sitting on wood blocks in the room. Ole was sitting behind a sawed-wood desk. They all jumped to their feet.

Tom crossed the room. "At ease, everyone but Master Sergeant Ole Swensen."

Tom walked over in front of Ole. Wearing as stern a look as he could muster, Tom faced Ole almost nose to nose. Sergeant Swensen, you've been wearing those stripes for some time now. I was at least partly responsible for your getting them. I have to tell you now that it is my duty to take them away. I want you to take off that uniform coat and throw it to Sergeant Bascomb. He might be able to use it."

Ole looked nonplussed, and his face got long as he stared at Tom. He took off his coat and threw it to Bascomb. Next, Tom handed Ole a folded-up coat he had been carrying. Sergeant Swensen, I have been authorized by Colonel Brewster to order you to put this one on."

Ole looked further confused. He looked at Tom questioningly, but he did put the coat on.

Tom smiled. "Lieutenant Swensen, my congratulations! You are not only the newest lieutenant in the outfit; you are now the reservation Indian Agent." All the soldiers in the room started clapping and clustered around Ole, slapping him on the back and congratulating him.

After a time, Ole dismissed the soldiers, and he and Tom moved to a couple of blocks and sat talking. Ole took off the coat and looked at the bars on the shoulders. "Ay never thought Ay'd see those t'ings on a coat of mine. Vat kind of hold did you have on the Colonel to get him to do this?"

"Actually, it was his idea."

"Vy am Ay the Indian Agent? Vat are you going to do?"

"I've been assigned to the fort. Adjutant for the colonel. I'm not sure how I'm going to like it. I won't be out scrounging around the countryside with the likes of you, but if I'm going to be a married man, maybe it is better this way."

"Ay have been vondering vat you said to that girl. She has sure been moping around here since she got back. You'd better go talk to her."

"I'm going to get with her right after supper. What's wrong?"

"Ay don't know. Anyhow, Ay'll get my stuff out of your room so you can bring your soogans in."

"No. You are the Agent now. That's your room. I'll spread out in the barracks."

Gray Dove was waiting when Tom arrived at the teepee. She came out of the entry and took Tom's hand. They walked down their favorite trail to the pine tree. Gray Dove had her head down staring at the trail as they walked. Tom could sense that she was not her usual cheerful self, and went along with her need for silence.

When they were seated against the pine, Tom waited for a while for her to speak, and finally said, "Gray Dove, what's the matter? You are very quiet, and I can tell not very happy. Have I done something?"

"Tom, when you left, we were planning to get married at the fort. Tom, I love you very much, but I can't do it."

"Why not? What has happened? You were all right when I left. Everything was fine. You can't mean that!"

"Yes. I've thought it through and through. I just don't fit in that place. The ladies look on me as an outsider, or something, and I don't have their fine manners. I would be an embarrassment to you when we went there. I couldn't stand that!"

"You would never embarrass me! I am so proud of you. But there is something else I have to tell you. I've been made Colonel Brewster's adjutant and I'll be stationed at the fort."

"Oh, that is even worse! They would never accept me as the adjutant's wife."

Tom was thunderstruck! How could this be happening? He had been so looking forward to being with her. He had been building dreams about their life together. He felt like he had been hit with a sledgehammer. "You can't mean that, Gray Dove. I love you very much. I have been dreaming of our life together. I thought you and Rosalyn got along fine. She told me before I left the fort, that she liked you very much and was looking forward to our wedding."

"Yes, I like Rosalyn. She is nice. It was the other ladies mostly."
"What did they say to you? Were they mean?"

"No, I could just feel what they were thinking. Tom, I was raised as an Indian, I am used to their ways, and I feel that this is where I belong. I'm just not good for you."

They talked on into the night, and she resolutely stuck to her decision. Tom did his best to dissuade her, but she was adamant. Finally, she asked Tom to take her back to the teepee.

Tom went back to the Agency building and crawled into his soogans. His heart was heavy, and his thoughts black.

The next day Tom tried to see Gray Dove, but she wouldn't talk to him. He wandered around the compound, trying to think of a way to convince her. If she wouldn't even see him, it was going to be hard.

Two more days passed. Tom spent most of his time with Ole, dumping his dark thoughts on his best friend. Ole sympathized but wasn't able to do much to cheer Tom up. The time that it had taken him to get here and the time he had to allow to get back to the fort just about used up what time he had left to convince Gray Dove she was wrong. He even had thoughts about grabbing her and running off. He just had to do something!

A few days after Gray Dove had refused Tom's entreaties, Pretty Rose was holding Gray Dove's hand as they walked beside the creek. "You can't mean it! You've been moping around for a month now, and terribly unhappy. You're wrong! You know he loves you, and you know you love him. What does it matter what other people think? What do you want? Most women would be the happiest with that life."

"I just know I would ruin his career. All those Army wives are so well-mannered, and proper, and I feel like they are looking down their noses at me. He has been promoted to adjutant and we would be living in the fort. I couldn't do that to him."

"What does he say?"

"He says he loves me and wants to get married like we were planning."

"You're crazy. I think I am going to beat you with a big stick and see if there still is a brain in that silly head of yours. Besides that, you are ruining my life."

"How am I ruining your life?"

"I was thinking that when you go to the fort for your wedding, I would tell that big Swede of mine that we should go along and do the same thing at the same time. It might get him in the right frame of mind. Now if you really care for me, you will straighten up and tell your soldier that you have finally seen the light."

"Do you really think I should? That I wouldn't ruin his future? You always tell me the right thing, and I want so much to think you are right."

Pretty Rose gave her a push. "Go up there right now and tell him! If you don't I won't even be your friend any more, for what you are doing to me." She laughed. "Go do it."

Tom was deep in thought. It was coming time he had to go back to the fort, and Gray Dove wouldn't even see him. He had to come up with some way to get to talk to her, and convince her to change her mind. He left the Agency building and decided to walk down to the creek. He might think better down there. It was always his refuge to go over problems.

As he approached the creek, he spotted Pretty Rose and Gray Dove coming toward him. He stopped and waited for them. Maybe this was his chance to get to talk to her.

Pretty Rose saw him, left Gray Dove, and came running up. "Tom, Gray Dove has something she wants to say to you."

Gray Dove walked up and took Tom's hand. "Tom, I'm sorry that I've been so silly. I really am not very sure of myself - of what I should do. Pretty says I'm crazy for the way I feel. I don't want to hurt you or your career. I love you very much. She says to go with my heart. What should I do?"

"There is no question! You should marry me at the very first opportunity. I'll throw the first woman that makes a snide remark about you into boiling oil, and then skin her alive. I think you are mistaken about those women, though. You will find they are mostly all much like Rosalyn, and you like her. Besides, she told me that she almost had your wedding dress finished. You can't disappoint her like that."

Gray Dove broke into tears. She stepped forward and put her arms around him and cried uncontrollably for a time. "Thank you, Tom. I love you so much."

They walked back to the pine tree and sat with their arms around each other far into the night.

Pushing his way through the office door, Tom met Ole just coming out of his room. "Mister Agent. I want to requisition a team and wagon for a short time. If I'm not mistaken, I won't have to look for a driver to bring the wagon back. Any truth to that?"

"Ya, Ay've got my orders. I don't know, Tom. Vat vould the colonel say? He yust put me in the yob and I take time to go to the fort! Pretty vants to go get married at the same time as Gray Dove, and at the fort. Vat do you t'ink Ay should do? Ay told her Ay vanted to marry her, but Ay didn't say how soon. Ay don't know vat Ay should do."

"Ole, I'm glad for you. Pretty is a great girl. Tell her to pack up her things, and if I were you, I'd have her bring her parents along, too. I think we can make room for them. Gray Dove is bringing her parents. I'd like to leave tomorrow morning. My leave is getting short. I'll talk to Brewster when I get back about your coming along. Bascomb can handle things here for a couple of days. I had the devil's own time convincing Gray Dove we should get married now. She was afraid she wouldn't fit in at the fort."

CHAPTER SIXTEEN

Tom arranged blankets in the back of the wagon where the young women and their parents could rest comfortably on the way to the fort. He put in enough supplies for their meals during the trip, and saw to their breakfast early the next morning. That finished, he loaded everyone aboard, he and Ole climbed up on the seat, and he flicked the reins, starting the team on its way.

Stealing glances back every now and then, Tom could see Gray Dove and Pretty Rose hunkered down in a blanket talking up a storm, which he guessed might have something to do with the coming weddings. Maple Leaf and Pretty's mother were doing much the same. Chief Capture was watching the scenery go by.

A small stream crossed their path about mid-morning and Tom stopped the team and helped everyone out to stretch their legs. Before going on, he and Ole brought water from the stream for everyone, and he let the horses drink as they crossed the water.

At noon they stopped on the edge of the timber for lunch. This was about the end of the timber and it would be open prairie land from now on. After they had eaten, Tom lifted Pretty up to the seat and told Ole to drive. He climbed into the back with Gray Dove and the others and they proceeded out onto the prairie land.

Tom rode with his arm around Gray Dove, and they discussed for hours on end what living would be like at the fort. She still had some misgivings, and he tried his best to assure her that it was going to be all right.

Crossing a small creek just before dusk, Ole pulled up under the shade of some cottonwood trees, and they made camp for the night. Tom broke out the jerky, biscuits, and brought up water for everyone, while Maple Leaf and Pretty's mother warmed some beans and Gray Dove made coffee. Tom and Gray Dove took a stroll along the stream before turning in to their blankets for the night.

The next three days were much the same. Endless miles across the prairie, with stops along the way to eat and sleep. But it was the best trek over that stretch of ground that Tom and Ole had ever taken, thanks to the presence of Gray Dove and Pretty.

On the afternoon of the fourth day, Tom stopped the team and pointed out into the distance. The fort stood in stark relief on a far hilltop. "We'll just about make it by dark. We'll just keep going until we get there, so as to have daylight to travel in."

Wheeling the wagon toward the headquarters building, Tom pulled up at the hitch rail in front. Rosalyn Brewster came running out, and when Tom helped Gray Dove out of the wagon, the two women hugged each other heartily. Gray Dove introduced Pretty, her mother, and Maple Leaf to Rosalyn, and all the women walked into the building.

Colonel Brewster came out of his office. "Hello, Tom. Glad you're back. Hello, Swensen. I didn't expect you. Is anything wrong at the reservation?"

Tom spoke up. "No, Sir, I told him I was sure it would be all right. It seems that Pretty Rose has some plans for him that involve a wedding. I told him that Bascomb could take care of things for a couple of weeks. Everything seemed to be well under control at the reservation."

"Of course. The ladies can use our spare bedrooms, and the men can bunk with you, Tom. Take the men to your quarters and the horses to the livery barn, and I'll see you and Swensen when you get done."

Brewster waved Tom and Ole to some chairs when they entered his office. "Congratulations on your promotion, Swensen. If I had known you would be here so soon, I would have waited to give it to you and had a ceremony to go with it. From all I hear, you are doing a good job there on the reservation."

"Thank you, Sir. Ay'm doing the best Ay know how. Probably not as good as Tom did."

"Well, keep up the good work. Tom, we brought in another bunch of Sioux yesterday. I think there are enough to start another reservation now." He pulled a map from his desk drawer, and pointed to a colored section in the middle of the map. "This is the area I have picked out. I haven't been there, and I want you to go take a look and see if it is satisfactory. This next week you and I will go over the records of some soldiers that we can assign to run it. I'd like to take the ones from your reservation. They are experienced, but it may be too soon to take them away yet."

"I'd like to suggest that we at least take Bascomb. He knows the ropes and he will make things happen for whoever is in charge. One of the others could take Bascomb's place."

"If Ay could make a suggestion - vy don't you put Bascomb in charge of the reservation? He knows how to set vun up. He vas there for the last vun."

"Tom, it's your decision. The reservations are your responsibility from now on."

"I think Ole has an excellent idea. Bascomb knows as much as we do about it, and he can get things done. All I can add is that he should get his bars. He has surely earned them."

"All right. I'm going to have to quit this business. I'm running out of Lieutenants' bars. I'll be hearing from the War Department one of these days. They'll think we're all officers and no men out here. I will say, though, that every one of you has more than earned it.

"Tom, we need to get the new reservation going as soon as possible. I know you have a lot of other things that need attention, but we need to start."

"How much money do I have to work with? One thing that is going to be essential will be heated quarters for the Indians and the soldiers. Winter will be on them before they hit the ground. We at least had some time to get buildings up; they won't, and they will need some shelters and a way to heat them until they can get permanent buildings. Also, Ole will need to send Bascomb here to the fort as soon as he gets back there. He can start getting things going from here."

"I'll go over the money end with you soon."

After they left Brewster, Tom put his arm on Ole's shoulder. "I hate to take Bascomb away from you. I know you depend on him as much as I did, but he has earned the opportunity. I'm going to go look over the new reservation Indians. See if I can find a leader, and an interpreter. That will give us a leg up when Bascomb gets here. Want to come along?"

"No, Ay t'ink Ay'll go see if Ay can find Pretty."

"Good luck. The last time I tried to see Gray Dove, I nearly got handed my head. We men weren't allowed to see the finery they were dressing the women in until the ceremony. I'll see you at the quarters if you're still alive."

Tom walked over to the compound. It was a fenced-in area inside one end of the fort. It had a covered area at one side. Benches and tables had been installed for the Indians' use. A water pump was near the end of the last table. They had been issued blankets, and they were spread on the ground beyond the pump. It was obvious that they had no more to live with than those that he had taken to his reservation. Bascomb was going to have his work cut out for him.

Tom had the guard let him into the compound, and he walked in among the Indians. He couldn't see any one that he could identify as a chief. He was going to have to find the interpreter first and maybe he could point out the chief.

Tom walked around through the crowd. They all just stared at him, and conversation ceased as he approached. He would call out every so often. "Does anyone speak English?" He repeated it as he continued around the compound.

Looking them over as he walked, he spotted a young man that looked different somehow. He had dark hair and eyes, and was nearly as brown as the others, but something about his looks struck Tom.

Tom walked over to the young man. "Do you speak English?"

The man just looked at him without changing facial expression. Tom asked again, "Do you speak English?"

Tom thought he could see a flicker in the young man's eyes that might mean he could understand the question. "Young fellow, if you can understand English you could be a big help to your people here. They are going to need someone who can tell us what their needs are as we go along. If you can speak English, please let me know. Your people will appreciate it."

Tom and the man stared into each other's eyes for a time. The man shifted his feet, looked around at the Indians who had crowded around him, and then back at Tom. "I speak English."

Tom breathed a sigh of relief. At least they would have a way of communicating. That was a big step! "Good. I need you to be the voice for your people. You can relate to them what we want them to do, and at the same time, if any of them need help, you can let me know. It will make things a lot easier for them if you will do that."

"I will do that."

"Come with me, then. I want to talk to you."

Tom led him out of the compound, past the guard, and over to his quarters. Once inside, Tom pointed to a chair on one side of the table and he sat across from him.

"What are you called?"

"I am called White Eagle"

"All right, White Eagle. My name is Tom. We are going to move all of you to a reservation, help you set it up so that you can live in peace, and hopefully we will be friends when it is all done. A man by the name of Bascomb will be your leader. He is a kind man, and will do his best to make things good for all of your people.

"He will need you to take messages back and forth between him and your people. You will like him when you get to know him."

"I will carry his messages."

"Next, I need to know who your chief is. We need to have someone who can speak for all of your people."

"My father is the chief. He is Sitting Buffalo. He can speak for all."

"Good. Will you tell him what we have planned when you return to the stockade? I will want to get together with him and you soon."

"I will tell him."

"How is it that you can speak English?"

"My white parents were killed when I was very young. I was captured and taken by the Indians. My father took me into his teepee."

"Who were your white parents? What was your white name?"

"My parents called me Bobby."

"Do you remember your last name?"

"I'm not sure - maybe Madden or something."

"Madden? Could it have been Madison?"

"Maybe."

"Madison! Did you have an older sister? Was her name Ruth?"

"Yes, yes, her name was Ruth. I remember…."

Tom jumped to his feet. He grabbed the man by his arm. "Come with me. I think your sister is right across the parade grounds there."

He almost ran, pulling the young man along behind him. He ran up on the porch into the colonel's front office, and over to the door of his quarters. He pounded on the door, and rushed in when Rosalyn opened it.

"Where is Gray Dove? I need to see her!"

Hearing the noise, Gray Dove came into the room, followed by Pretty. "Tom, what is it?"

"Honey, I think this is your brother! His parents were captured when he was young, and he had an older sister named Ruth. It can't be anything else. White Eagle, I think this is your sister."

Tom stepped back and let them absorb this news and look each other over.

Gray Dove put a hand to her throat. She looked at the man, then at Tom. "Tom, are you sure? Can it really be?"

She walked over to the young man, looking at him intently. "Are you really Bobby Madison?"

A smile came on the young man's face. "Yes, that was my white name."

"I can't believe it, after all this time! Come over here, let's get acquainted." She led him to a couple of chairs. The others pulled back and left them alone.

Tom went to the commissary and obtained a set of clothing for Bobby. He felt sure now that the man was, in fact, Gray Dove's brother. He got some blankets for him, as well, and brought it all to his quarters.

After several hours, Tom returned to the colonel's private quarters and entered as Rosalyn opened the door for him. "Is everything all right?"

"Everything's fine, Tom. Come in."

Gray Dove saw him, jumped to her feet, and ran over and put her arms around him. "Oh, Tom, he is my brother! He really is! I never thought I would see him again. I'm so happy."

"I'm glad, Honey. I'm glad you're together again. I hope that he feels the same."

"He does, Tom. I can tell."

Rosalyn came over. "This is a celebration, Tom. We'll expect you and Ole for supper."

Tom looked at Gray Dove. "I have a set of clothes for him over at our quarters. If I can have him for a little bit, we'll start the transformation."

"I hate to let him out of my sight, but go ahead, and hurry back!"

Tom led Bobby back to his quarters where they both cleaned up, and Bobby got acquainted with his new white folks clothing. It all seemed strange to him, but he went along with it. He was overjoyed at finding his sister again.

Bobby was seated between Gray Dove and Tom at the supper table that night, and though he felt really uncomfortable at the table, he followed Tom's and Gray Dove's leads and managed pretty well. The food seemed strange to him, and the formality was different than he was used to, but it was worth it to him to be with his sister again.

That night, after they had eaten, Tom took Bobby back to his quarters. "Bobby, I am so glad you found your sister, and she is beside herself.

"I have been thinking what to do for the future. I know you have grown up hating the pony soldiers, and you may not want to do this, but if you are willing, I will talk to the colonel about making you a scout for the fort here.

"Your Indian family and the others are going to need you to interpret for them while they are setting up the reservation. Most of the soldiers that are sent there will come back in six months or so. I think you should go with them and be their interpreter, then come back with the soldiers, and stay here as a scout. That way you could be close to your sister most of the time. Would you be willing to do that?"

"You want me to be a pony soldier? What would my people say?"

"I think they will be friends with the pony soldiers before long. They became friendly on the reservation we just set up. Not only that, the colonel can use your ability as a tracker when you are a scout. Also, you will have some time to say goodbye to your Indian family while you are at the new reservation. I'm sure you will be able to go back for visits with them."

Bobby sat staring at the floor for a long time.

"All right. My sister says I can trust you. I'll do it."

Now, Tom thought, all I have to do is convince Gray Dove that her brother should go to the new reservation, then, convince the colonel that he should take Bobby on as a scout and Gray Dove would be able to see him often. Maybe this is what adjutants do.

CHAPTER SEVENTEEN

EPILOGUE

Lieutenant Olaf Swensen stood resplendent in his new uniform with bars on the shoulders next to Captain Thomas Colter, while across the altar stood the very best man, Colonel Charles Brewster, and the very best matron of honor, Rosalyn Brewster, as they all gazed down the aisle at the beautiful Gray Dove on the arm of a beaming Chief Horse Capture, followed by the lovely Pretty Rose, escorted by her father. The front row was occupied by a smiling Maple Leaf, dressed up in her new flowery dress given her by her soon-to-be-son-in-law, and the equally happy mother of Pretty Rose, Yellow Butterfly. Bobby sat next to them in his new finery with a smile on his face.

The Chaplain, newly out of Seminary, nervously waiting to perform his first wedding, fumbled with the pages he had marked in the book.